The Michaelmas Murders

a&b

The Michaelmas Murders

MANDY MORTON

Allison & Busby Limited
12 Fitzroy Mews
London W1T 6DW
allisonandbusby.com

First published in Great Britain by Allison & Busby in 2017.

Copyright © 2017 by MANDY MORTON

A CIP catalogue record for this book is available from
the British Library.

First Edition

ISBN 978-0-7490-2113-9

Typeset in 11.5/16.5 pt Sabon by
Allison & Busby Ltd.

The paper used for this Allison & Busby publication
has been produced from trees that have been legally sourced
from well-managed and credibly certified forests.

Printed and bound by
CPI Group (UK) Ltd, Croydon, CR0 4YY

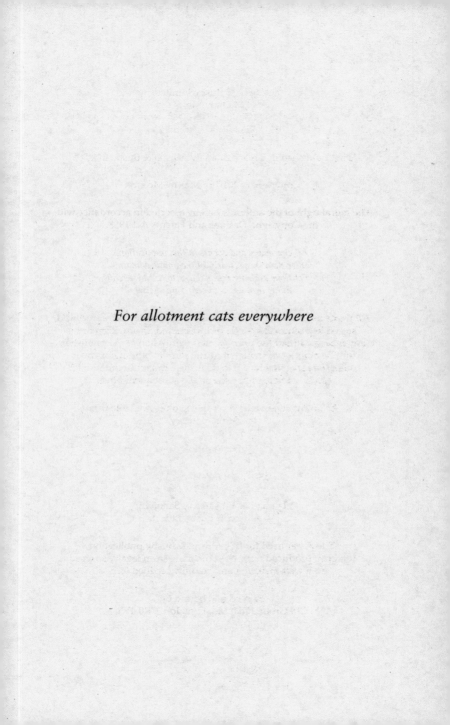

For allotment cats everywhere

CHAPTER ONE

Bonny Grubb and Fluff Wither-Fork stared down at the dead cat. 'I ain't seen 'im round 'ere before,' said Bonny, giving the body an exploratory nudge with her garden boot. ''E's not done much for me onion patch, either, Miss. 'E weren't there yesterdee, when I done some weedin'.'

'Well, the fact is he's here now, Bonny, and judging by the look of him, he's clearly been murdered.'

'On account of 'im 'avin' is 'ead bashed in, Miss?'

'Yes, Bonny – and I would think that the rock lying next to him had a great deal to do with it.'

The sarcasm in Fluff Wither-Fork's reply passed Bonny by in her keenness to assess the damage to her onions. Some lay half out of the soil, others were trampled beyond recognition, and all were tainted by the blood of the corpse that lay stretched out in the contorted throws of his final moments. The early-morning sun shone on the body, giving life to his jacket as steam rose from the damp clothing.

''E 'as the look of a compost 'eap, all steamin' like that,' observed Bonny, breaking the silence.

Fluff, who usually enjoyed her Gypsy tenant's views on life, shook off the prospect of any further conversation by heading back up the allotment. When she reached the gate, she turned back to bark out an order. 'Cover him up with some sacking and tell no one of this. Leave everything just as it is, Bonny. I'm calling in the professionals.' In no mood to wait for a reply, Fluff Wither-Fork snapped the gate shut behind her and strode off in the direction of Wither-Fork Hall.

Bonny Grubb stared after her, bereft at the realisation that her onions would not be winning any rosettes at the Michaelmas Flower and Produce Show this year. She returned to her caravan and hauled an old sack out from under the wheels; dragging it back up the allotment, she threw it over her unwanted visitor, then returned to her caravan to fry sausages on her stove and await the professionals that her landlady had promised.

CHAPTER TWO

The No. 2 Feline Detective Agency had been closed for two whole weeks, as Hettie Bagshot and her friend and chief assistant, Tilly Jenkins, were treating themselves to a late summer holiday. The agency, which they ran from the back of Betty and Beryl Butter's pie and pastry shop on the town's high street, had clocked up enough assignments across the spring and summer months to make the holiday affordable.

The two tabbies had spent a week on their friend Poppa's narrowboat, exploring the cuisine on offer at every riverside hostelry that the waterways could offer, and transferring at the end of their first week to a holiday camp by the sea, where Hettie had developed sunburnt ears and Tilly had won first prize in the clock golf competition. The two friends had enjoyed every minute of their time away, adding pounds to their tabby waistlines as their pockets grew emptier – but now, the holiday was well and truly over, and their much depleted coffers meant that they would have to get back to work as soon as possible.

The rent on their office, which doubled as a small but comfortable home, was due any minute, and although the Butters charged very little and threw in coal and luncheon vouchers to be exchanged in their bakery, Hettie and Tilly knew that the debt would have to be paid on time. Hettie sat on her fireside chair, still in her dressing gown, cleaning the remains of a cheese triangle from her whiskers as Tilly hauled their office phone out of the staff sideboard. 'We should have a listen to the answerphone,' she said. 'I hope I connected it up properly before we left.'

'Well, you certainly wasted enough money phoning it up every day. All that palaver we had over trying to find a telephone box that worked.'

'I just wanted to make sure that everything was all right at home,' said Tilly, engaging a logic which – as usual – made no sense to anyone but her.

Hettie was tempted to explore the concept further, but no sooner had she opened her mouth to speak than the answerphone sprang into life. The first message was a little distant, but Tilly's voice was unmistakable: 'Hello,

Tilly here. We're having a lovely time on Poppa's boat and we're cooking sprats for lunch in the galley – that's what Poppa calls his kitchen, although it's not a proper kitchen, it's really one gas ring plugged into a big gas bottle. We're having our tea at the Shove and Halfpenny later if Hettie can manage the lock gates. Poppa says she's a—' At this point the answering machine appeared to cut Tilly off with a bleep and moved on to the next message. 'Hello, Tilly here. Forgot to say, Poppa caught a very large fish today. He's having it stuffed as he says it's the biggest fish he's ever caught. Hettie wanted to eat it, but Poppa says a big one like that doesn't come along every day and he's putting it on display in his salon – that's what he calls his sitting room on the boat, although it's not really a sitting r—' Once again the answering machine bleeped, bringing Tilly's appraisal of Poppa's living quarters to an abrupt end.

Tilly had settled down on her blanket by the fire, enthralled by her audio postcards. More than a little irritated by Tilly's new-found friendship with the machine, Hettie attempted to bring matters to a head by reaching for the pause button before Tilly could continue with her travel log. 'How many messages did you leave on that thing?' she asked. 'It's supposed to be for prospective clients.'

Upset by Hettie's lack of enthusiasm, Tilly pressed the fast-forward button, promising herself a catch-up with her own messages later. 'It says we have twenty-nine messages, but I'm certain that I only left 28 – two for each day of our holiday. So there's one spare.'

Hettie resisted the temptation to put the answerphone and Tilly back in the staff sideboard, and quickly ran through the messages, fast-forwarding to the final one; according to the time and date setting, it had come in earlier that morning when both cats were still fast asleep. At the sound of a very different and somewhat authoritative cat, Hettie and Tilly drew closer to the machine and the dulcet tones of Fluff Wither-Fork, the town's most illustrious landowner, filled their ears. 'This is an urgent message from Fluff Wither-Fork for the No. 2 Feline Detectives. There has been a murder on my allotments, and I would appreciate your attendance at Wither-Fork Hall at your earliest convenience.' The caller rang off and the answering machine added a series of bleeps, signalling that it had no further messages to offer.

Hettie threw off her dressing gown as Tilly clapped her paws. 'Just in time for the rent, and it sounds like a nice murder to get our teeth into,' she said, springing to the bottom drawer of the filing cabinet to choose a cardigan suitable for the case.

'I'm not sure there's such a thing as a *nice* murder,' said Hettie, pulling on her business slacks. 'If we get a move on, we should catch the ten-thirty bus from outside the post office. It's a bloody nuisance that Bruiser has chosen this week to go fishing with Poppa.

We're going to have to rely on public transport.'

Tilly nodded, saddened by the fact that Miss Scarlet, their motorbike and sidecar, was out of action; their friend Bruiser was the only cat who could drive it. 'I suppose Bruiser's entitled to a holiday,' she said wistfully, as she took her best mac down from the back of the door.

CHAPTER THREE

The town's bus service could never be described as reliable. Even those cats lucky enough to catch a bus in the first place had no guarantee that they would reach their destination on time, or in some cases at all. The main problem was breakdowns, due partly to the age of the buses and partly to a lack of maintenance. The depot at the back of Malkin and Sprinkle's department store boasted a large garage that housed two buses and an assortment of spare parts, all taken from the original fleet of six as they gradually ground to a halt on routes in and out of the town. There was no money to replace them, but the cheerful and optimistic staff of four did their best to make several journeys each day up and down the high street. Breakdowns had become a regular feature on Clippy Lean's route, so the town's bus conductress of the year had taken steps to ensure that there was plenty of on-board entertainment for her passengers to enjoy should they become victims of an unscheduled delay. She had placed an assortment of board games and jigsaws in the luggage racks above each seat, and on cold days she procured a number of hot-water bottles, which she filled from the bus's radiator as it boiled over the silent engine. Clippy loved her job and would do anything to keep her customers happy.

Hettie and Tilly only had to wait ten minutes before the bus loomed into view. The fact that this was the 9.30 service, arriving at 10.40, didn't concern them as they clambered aboard, enjoying a royal welcome from Clippy, who regarded them as local celebrities thanks to a number of headline-grabbing cases. The bus coughed and lurched its way down the high street, and Clippy made unsteady progress up the aisle to the back seat, where Hettie and Tilly had settled themselves. 'Two returns to Wither-Fork Hall please,' said Tilly, proffering a pawful of change.

Clippy dispensed two pink tickets from her machine, which she wore with pride strapped across her chest. 'I'm not sure how far up Wither-Fork Hill we'll go today, so I'll just take for two singles to save me having to issue a refund. We've already had a boil-over and a fan belt incident this morning, and I'm thinking that Wither-Fork Hill just might break the camel's back.'

The bus made an unscheduled stop outside Meridian Hambone's hardware store, and Clippy skipped back down the aisle to welcome aboard the Gamp sisters, who did everything in unison. The sisters carried identical bags, and wore identical coats and wellingtons, and spoke as one to order their tickets, synchronising the opening and closing of their purses to perfection. They, too, were headed for Wither-Fork Hall, where they worked one of the allotments at the top of the town.

Several more stops came and went without incident, and by the time the bus had reached the foot of Wither-Fork Hill, Hettie and Tilly were feeling almost confident of reaching its summit. Reality struck halfway up the steep incline with a hissing and bubbling noise, followed by a rhythmic banging from the back of the bus where the engine lived – or, at this point, died.

'Sorry, everybody,' said Clippy, apologetically. 'This is as far as we're going at the moment. If you're in a hurry, I suggest you leg it from here. For those of you who'd rather stay on board, there's lots of games to keep you happy. I'm off shift for an hour, so I'm going to lift some spuds while we're waiting for the mechanic.'

Clippy abandoned her ticket machine in a locker at the front of the bus. She collected a spade and an empty sack from the suitcase hold, swapped her sandals for a pair of heavy gardening boots, then set off up the hill towards the allotments, whistling a cheerful tune. The Gamp sisters followed at a much slower pace, and Hettie and Tilly – pulling up their mac collars against the threat of rain – puffed their way up the hill towards Wither-Fork Hall, leaving the rest of the passengers to their backgammon, tiddlywinks, and snakes and ladders.

At the top of the hill, to the left, was a substantial parkland where Wither-Fork Hall nestled in baronial splendour; to the right, a gate led through to the allotments. Catching her breath from the exertions of the hill, Hettie watched as Clippy Lean and the Gamps made their way down the central path, peeling off onto their designated patches of land. She was no stranger to the allotments: she had, in one of her past lives, lived on a plot there until her shed with a bed was taken in the great storm. Shortly afterwards, the Butters had offered her sanctuary in their old storeroom at the bakery, which had now become a permanent home for her and more recently Tilly, who had never had a proper home until Hettie befriended her.

'I hope we can solve this murder quickly,' said Tilly. 'I'm not sure I could climb up here too often. I don't know how the allotment cats manage.'

'Most of them live on the allotments,' said Hettie. 'There's some sort of ancient entitlement connected to Wither-Fork Hall, if my memory serves me well – sitting tenants with vegetables, or some such nonsense. I spent a summer up here in an abandoned shed. So did Bruiser. No one seemed to mind until the storm came and did for us. Several of the older cats died that night when their sheds collapsed around them. I was one of the lucky ones. It was this time of year, actually – they had to cancel the Michaelmas Flower and Produce Show out of respect. That, and the fact that the storm had taken all the vegetables.'

Tilly stifled a giggle at the thought of a legion of flying beetroot, carrots and cauliflowers heading down Wither-Fork Hill towards the town. 'I hope we can go to the Mickeymouse Show this year. I think it's next weekend.'

'That depends on this murder, I suppose,' said Hettie, as they approached the gatehouse. 'They hold the show in the grounds in front of the Hall – and it's *Michaelmas*, not Mickeymouse! After the saint.'

'I always preferred Minnie, anyway,' said Tilly, threatening to take the conversation in a completely different direction, which Hettie had the sense to ignore.

The gatehouse was a sizeable property made of red brick, rising to miniature turrets that stood clear of the roof at each corner. It looked like a small castle, and stood as guardian to the main entrance of Wither-Fork Hall. The gates to the driveway were firmly shut, and Hettie pulled on an iron bell pull to attract attention. There was no instant reply, so she tried again.

'Ahoy there!' came a voice from nowhere. 'What can I do for you?'

Hettie and Tilly moved closer to the gates and peered through the bars, trying to locate the voice.

'Hello!' came the voice again. 'I'm up here!' Hettie stepped back and looked up at the roof of the gatehouse, where she found the voice and the cat it belonged to leaning out over one of the turrets and training a pair of binoculars on them. 'Captain Micks Wither-Spoon at your service. How can I help?'

Hettie responded in her official tone. 'I am Hettie Bagshot from the No. 2 Feline Detective Agency, and this is my assistant, Tilly Jenkins. We have an appointment with Miss Wither-Fork.'

'Is that the "as was" or the "as is" Miss Wither-Fork?'

Hettie – already confused by the fork and spoon issue – was becoming more than a little irritated by the keeper of the gate, who seemed to be talking in riddles. 'I'm sorry, Mr Wither-Spoon, but I don't know what you mean. All I know is that Miss Wither-Fork is expecting us regarding an urgent matter, and if you'd be kind enough to open the gates we can go about our business at Wither-Fork Hall.'

'That's all very well,' replied the cat on the turret, 'but I wouldn't be doing my job if I let every Tom, Dick and Harry in, would I? And it very much depends on whether you want the "as is" or the "as was", because the "as was" Wither-Fork lives here with me at the gatehouse and is now a Wither-Spoon, and the "as is" Wither-Fork lives at the Hall. Or to put it plainer – do you want to see Fluff or Mash?'

Tilly giggled as Hettie's hackles rose above her upturned collar. 'My business is with Miss *Fluff* Wither-Fork and is a matter of life and death. I have no interest in speaking with anyone else at this point, so would you kindly let us in?'

Micks Wither-Spoon moved grudgingly away from the turret and appeared several minutes later by the gates, unlocking them from the inside. Hettie and Tilly swept through, noting that the gatekeeper was dressed in some sort of bizarre costume left over from the Napoleonic Wars, with a cutlass jammed in his belt, a three-cornered hat on his head, and a row of medals splayed across his chest. The overall effect was ridiculous rather than authoritative, and the two cats made sure to put a safe distance between him and them before bursting into peals of laughter.

The driveway to the Hall was long, and it gave them an opportunity to pull themselves together. 'That gatekeeper is a bloody lunatic!' Hettie observed shrewdly. 'And is he saying that he's married a Wither-Fork, who's now a Wither-Spoon, called Mash?'

'I wonder if they have a gardener called Spread Wither-Knife?' added Tilly, and the two friends collapsed into another bout of laughter, which was only brought under control at the steps of Wither-Fork Hall.

The door was opened before Hettie had even considered lifting the heavily decorated knocker. Fluff Wither-Fork must have watched their progress up the driveway and was ready to receive them, dressed for the weather in a long trench coat and a pair of wellingtons. 'Welcome to Wither-Fork Hall,' she said. 'I assume you are from the No. 2 Feline Detective Agency, and before we go any further, let me apologise for any rudeness you received at the gatehouse. My sister's choice of life partner is a constant concern to me. Micks Wither-Spoon lives in a world of his own, harmless but completely unfathomable, and my poor sister Mash just laps up his imbecilic outbursts and sometimes even joins in. Last week they got themselves done up in doublet and hose, and performed a revised version of *Romeo and Juliet*, in which neither of them died. It received rapturous applause from a charabanc of visitors to my water gardens, but now they're threatening to give their *Macbeth* at the Michaelmas Show, and that's the last thing I need – especially as they intend to reverse the roles and let Micks wear a dress! Never a truer statement than "'tis better if it be done quickly". In fact, I could be tempted to run the pair of them through rather than suffer any more of their antics. If they had the cares and the worries that I have to put up with, they wouldn't have time to dress up and be so ridiculous. If Mash had been born two minutes earlier than me, I could be putting my paws up at the gatehouse and she would have to deal with the day-to-day nightmare of running an estate with no money and no help.'

Hettie and Tilly stood and waited for Fluff Wither-Fork's tale of woe to subside into something more manageable, before steering the conversation around to the reason they were there. It occurred to Hettie that Fluff Wither-Fork was heading rapidly to her wits' end, and a murder on her allotments was possibly the least of her worries. The realisation that she had poured out her troubles to two total strangers brought the landowner back down to her baronial front lawn, and, with only a slight hesitation, she rose to her full height, reinstating her nobility and bringing a little more decorum to the situation. 'I mustn't take up too much of your time, Miss er . . . ?'

'Bagshot. Hettie Bagshot and Tilly Jenkins,' responded Hettie in her most helpful tone.

'Yes, quite,' said Fluff. 'I think it best if you follow me to the allotments so that you can see for yourselves.'

She set out at a brisk pace down the drive, with

Hettie and Tilly doing their best to keep up. When they reached the gatehouse, Micks lurched into their path. 'You've got to say the password if you want me to open the gates.'

Fluff pushed him aside, turning the key in the lock herself and throwing the gates wide. 'I've no time for your idiotic behaviour today, Micks. Go and get that ridiculous outfit off, and leave these gates open until my guests and I return from the allotments. I don't know what your game is, but I'm in no mood to play along – and you can tell my sister that I wish to speak with her during lunch at the Hall. *You* are not invited.'

Crestfallen, Micks Wither-Spoon slunk back into the gatehouse, and Hettie and Tilly followed Fluff across the road and through the gate to the allotments.

CHAPTER FOUR

The Wither-Fork allotments were laid out in plots of equal size to the left and right of a central path. Fluff turned left into the first plot, which was dominated at the top end by a green Gypsy caravan with large red wheels. The chimney, which forced its way through the rounded roof, belched a plume of white smoke into the air, and Hettie's keen nose detected an unmistakable smell of sausages.

Fluff approached the caravan as Bonny Grubb emerged, wiping her whiskers on a large, dirty red handkerchief, which she'd tugged from around her neck. 'Bonny, I've brought some detectives to look at the body. Could you lead the way please?'

Bonny looked first at Tilly and then at Hettie, whom she recognised instantly. 'Well, I never expected to see you up 'ere agin. I 'eard you'd landed nicely on yer paws and got yerself a town residence in a posh bit of the high street. Seen you in the newspapers I stuff me old boots with to dry 'em out. Detective now, is it? Well I never! Gone are them days when you warmed yer paws round me campfire.'

'Thank you, Bonny,' said Fluff. 'We need to get on with this. It's not a social call.'

This time Bonny did as she was told, and led the way to her onion patch and the heap of sacking in the middle of it. 'There 'e is – not moved an inch, see? I covered 'im as you said, Miss, an' I ain't spoke a word of it to none of 'em, just like you told me.'

Fluff nodded her approval, and Hettie surveyed the scene before moving forward to lift the sacking. Tilly reached into her mac pocket for her notebook and pencil, and stood poised to take down anything interesting. Hettie looked closely at the dead cat and the carnage around it; there was no doubt that the bloodstained rock had been used in the attack. One side of the face was caved in, the fur matted with dried blood, and there were several teeth scattered around the head; the coat the cat wore was soaked from the overnight rain. Hettie noted that the clothes were of good quality, and the boots were certainly not suitable for the wear and tear of life on an allotment. She searched the pockets next and found nothing.

At last, she stood back from the body and looked at Bonny Grubb. 'Do you have any idea who he might be, Bonny?'

'I told Miss. I ain't never seen 'im till I found 'im in me onions this mornin'.'

'And you heard nothing in the night or early this morning?' insisted Hettie, noticing that Bonny had become a little agitated.

'I sleeps sound in me van. I always 'as a little tipple afore I lays me 'ead down – part of me medicinals.'

'You mean you were out for the count on that moonshine you brew,' said Hettie.

'Well, I gotta do something with me taters,' Bonny said, defensively.

'And what did you do with the contents of his pockets, Bonny?'

The Gypsy looked down at her boots as Fluff, Tilly and Hettie waited for an answer. 'I was goin' to tell, but that slipped me mind with the shock of me onions. I was 'opin' for a prize this year in the show, see, and I gets forgetful when I'm upset.'

Refusing to discuss Bonny Grubb's onions, Hettie repeated her question. This time, without any further excuse, Bonny led them back to her caravan and proffered a small bundle, which she had placed under her bunk mattress. 'That's all I got frum 'im – a few pennies and a pocketbook. No good ta me, as I ain't learnt me letters yet.'

Hettie took the book, but waved the pennies away. 'Compensation for your onions, Bonny. I'm sure Miss Wither-Fork is happy to let you keep them.'

Fluff shrugged her shoulders as if it was the last thing that was bothering her, and Bonny gleefully clawed the pennies back under her mattress.

'For decency's sake, I need to arrange to have the body removed,' Fluff said, addressing her remarks to Hettie as Tilly took charge of the pocketbook, mentally labelling it 'exhibit one' and checking that there was no name and address inside. 'Would that be all right? I can give Shroud and Trestle a ring when we get back to the Hall for lunch. I hope you'll both join me?'

Hettie thought for a moment, looking round at the other allotments and trying not to allow her unprofessional thoughts to stray to a slap-up meal at Wither-Fork Hall. 'At the moment, the onion patch is what we call a crime scene. Before the body is removed, I think the other allotment cats should come and view it – just in case anyone recognises him. Could you organise that, perhaps?'

Fluff nodded. 'That's a job for Jeremiah Corbit. He's a sort of unappointed overseer up here, and a bit of a rabble-rouser. I suppose he means well – a stickler for composting and such things. He lives two plots down. I'll go and ask him to round up the residents.'

She strode meaningfully back to the central path, while Bonny busied herself in her caravan and left Hettie and Tilly to kick their heels. 'So what do you think so far?' Tilly asked. 'Not much to go on, is there?'

'I'm more concerned about lunch,' grumbled Hettie. 'That cheese triangle has gone nowhere, and the memory of Bonny Grubb's breakfast sausages is too much. The whole allotment smells of them.'

Tilly dug deep into her mac pockets, triumphantly pulling out a custard cream, which had stuck to the lining. 'It's not much, but it might tide you over till we get back to Wither-Fork Hall.'

Hettie never ceased to be amazed by the resources that sprang from Tilly's pockets. She pounced gratefully on the biscuit, forcing it into her mouth as Fluff Wither-Fork returned with a short-haired grey, whiskery cat, and a colourful assortment of fellow allotment-holders. With regimental precision, the grey cat bullied the rest of the company into line ready for introductions, and Tilly stood by to write down the names in her notebook. Recognising the Gamp sisters and Clippy Lean, she entered their names first and marked them as non-residents who lived in the town. Jeremiah Corbit introduced himself with an air of importance, then reeled off the rest of the names. 'The Gamp sisters; Apple Chutney; Tarragon Trench; Gertrude Jingle; Desiree, Rooster and young Blight Chit; Dahlia and Gladys Mulch; and Clippy Lean. The only one missing is Blackberry Tibbs, and she works up at the Hall.'

Hettie took in a sea of expectant faces, all wondering why they had been wrenched from their allotments. When the names had been faithfully recorded in Tilly's notebook, she addressed them en masse. 'I am Hettie Bagshot and this is my assistant, Tilly Jenkins. We have been called in by Miss Wither-Fork to investigate a nasty death on Bonny Grubb's onion patch.' Hettie paused for effect, and the cats showed varying degrees of shock, horror and bewilderment before she continued, 'We need your help in identifying the body, so I would ask you all to follow me to the onion patch and take a close look.'

Hettie led the way, giving no warning of the state of the body and hoping that the element of surprise – or lack of it – might reveal the killer. Instead, she witnessed a united display of revulsion: the Gamps lost their breakfast in unison over Bonny Grubb's courgettes, and young Blight Chit wet himself in the middle of her elephant garlic. 'I'm sorry for the distress that this has caused you all,' Hettie said, 'but there is no doubt that this cat has been murdered. If any of you recognise him or have any information that will help us to find the killer, please come forward now.' She waited, but all the cats stood frozen to the spot. 'Very well. My assistant and I will visit you all individually on your allotments after lunch. In the meantime, perhaps you could take a look round your own plots for anything out of place or any signs of an intruder. I'm sure I don't need to tell you that you are all at risk until the killer has been apprehended.'

'What about the bus?' said Clippy Lean. 'I'm late on my shift already. I only popped up to dig some spuds, and I can't leave the passengers stranded halfway up Wither-Fork Hill.'

Hettie was now desperate for her lunch, and felt confident that the town's award-winning bus conductress was no killer; as Clippy didn't live on her allotment, she decided to let her rejoin the bus on the condition that Tilly could carry out a search of her patch and shed after lunch in her absence. Clippy happily agreed and returned to her plot to collect her potatoes and spade. The rest of the company dispersed, leaving Hettie, Tilly and Fluff to return to the Hall, where Hettie hoped for a big lunch before any further investigations were undertaken.

CHAPTER FIVE

From the outside, Wither-Fork Hall was a grand example of a Jacobean manor house. Facing back down an avenue of mature trees, the central part of the house was flanked by two high gabled wings, and Tilly amused herself by counting the windows that faced out across the parkland – eighteen in all, and none of them looking as if they'd been cleaned for several years.

Doing her best to keep pace with Fluff Wither-Fork's long and urgent strides, Hettie attempted some polite conversation. 'It's a lovely house,' she said. 'Have the Wither-Forks always been here?'

'Sadly, yes,' said Fluff. 'They managed to avoid all

the land-grabbing wars that raged around them over the centuries – dissolutions, civil wars, conquests. I'm not sure how they did it, but my ancestors always seemed to be looking the other way when trouble brewed. Their biggest problem was a tendency towards benevolence and an irritating belief that if you wrote it down and sealed it with wax the gift would last for ever.'

Hettie was curious to know more, but Fluff's assessment of her family tapered off as they reached the Hall, where the door was opened by an attractive, long-haired black and white cat wearing an apron over jogging bottoms and a T-shirt. 'Lunch is ready in the dining room, Miss. I'm afraid it's courgettes again.'

'Thank you, Blackberry. I'm sure you've done your best. Would you be kind enough to show Miss Bagshot and Miss Jenkins through to the dining room? I'll join them shortly after I've put in a call to Shroud and Trestle. There's been some unpleasantness on Bonny Grubb's onion patch that needs dealing with.'

Hettie smiled at Fluff's description of the murder, while Tilly stared open-mouthed at the size of the reception hall they found themselves in; it reminded her of those giant cathedrals where they buried kings and queens in stone coffins, although the only real point of interest in this particular example was a legion of galvanised buckets, which lined the hall like a guard of honour at a state occasion, strategically placed to take up the shortfall from roof tiles that were doing very little to keep out the rain. Fluff followed Tilly's gaze from the buckets to the badly stained plaster ceiling. 'Ah, I see you're already appreciating some of our finer points of interest. The buckets were introduced in my grandfather's time, and grow in number every year as the roof slates disintegrate. It's become an extreme sport to predict where the next bucket will be needed.'

As if leading a guided tour into another room, Fluff turned on her heel and strode off to call the town's undertakers. Hettie and Tilly followed the cat identified as Blackberry along the hall and into a vast and inhospitable dining room, whose giant wall-to-ceiling windows looked out over a vista of beautiful formal gardens: a rose parterre to the left; a considerable explosion of dahlias to the right; and a central walk of continuous fountains dancing off into the distance, arriving eventually at a series of small lily-clad ponds, which boasted a fine collection of statuary – cherubic cats, heraldic knights and weeping maidens, all staring down into the water.

'Those gardens prop the rest of the place up,' said Blackberry. 'Miss Wither-Fork totally relies on her garden tours, and without them we'd all be homeless. You can't live on vegetables alone.'

Hettie looked around her as Tilly headed towards a fireplace the size of a small bedsitting room, where a heatless fire smoked in the grate. The walls of the dining room were decorated with a mixture of faded tapestries and damp-riddled plaster, bulging from the walls as if trying to escape from the very fabric of the house. The dining table was long and surprisingly well polished, and there was a collection of odd chairs placed in an expectant clutch at the fire end of the room, apparently waiting for guests.

The only cheerful aspect of the room was an enormous bowl filled with dahlias of every colour and type; some boasted tiny sprays of daisy-like heads, others were large and spiky, shouting out their brilliance. The flowers were placed in the centre of the table and acted as a welcome distraction from the damp and decay that surrounded them.

'If you'd like to take your seats, I'll bring the pie in,' said Blackberry. 'I don't expect Miss Wither-Fork will be long, and she hates to be kept waiting for her food. I'll set off now if that's OK?'

Hettie smiled eagerly at Blackberry. 'That would be lovely, but it sounds like you've a distance to travel?'

'Ah well, it's ten minutes to the kitchen and back – down the stairs and right through the old staff quarters – and it's not easy to keep anything hot. That's why Miss Wither-Fork lives in the housekeeper's old parlour below stairs. It's next to the kitchen and much cosier than this barn of a place. We're in here today, though, as she has guests. She likes to keep up appearances, in spite of there being no money.'

Blackberry left the dining room and Hettie waited for her footsteps to die away on the flagstone floors before commenting on their surroundings. 'What a bloody nightmare!' she said, as she and Tilly settled themselves at the table. 'This huge house, all that land out there, a bunch of dependants up on the allotments, and a halfwit as a gatekeeper – you wouldn't want to be Fluff Wither-Fork for all the crispy batter bits in Elsie Haddock's chip shop.'

Tilly giggled. 'We haven't met the sister yet. I wonder what she's like.'

'All I'm interested in is the pie that Blackberry mentioned. If we've got to spend the afternoon up on the allotments, we'll need fortifying.'

'You'll need more than that,' said Fluff Wither-Fork as she strode into the dining room. Crossing to the fireplace, she hurled a log into the grate and took up her place at the head of the table, with Hettie and Tilly on either side. 'My tenants are a troublesome bunch of cats. As with most beneficiaries of charity, they take everything for granted as a God-given right. My hold on my house and land seems to exist solely for their benefit – and my personal reduced circumstances seem to reduce more and more as the years go by.'

'So why don't you sell up?' asked Hettie, keeping an eye on the door for Blackberry's return with the much-anticipated lunch.

'Oh, my dear Miss Bagshot – if only it were as

simple as that, I'd be long gone. The fact is, I'm stuck with it. If I walk away, what will happen? I can't sell out of the family, my sister wouldn't know where to start with running an estate of this size, and the covenant would be broken. No, I have no choice but to sit it out.'

Hettie was about to delve further into the Wither-Fork legacy when Blackberry Tibbs arrived, staggering under the weight of a very large pie. 'Sorry it took so long, Miss, but I had to rest it a couple of times on my way up.'

'Thank you, Blackberry. I'll deal with it from here. Would you collect the vegetables and deliver them to Malkin and Sprinkle? There are some white lilies from Gertrude Jingle, as well – we should get a good price for those. If you have any vegetables left over, they can go to the church for the harvest festival. That will be all for today. I expect you'll need to get on with your scarecrows.'

Hettie shot a questioning look at Tilly as Blackberry placed the pie in front of them, untied her apron and left the diners to their food. The pie, even by Betty and Beryl Butter's standards, looked magnificent. The pastry was golden brown and dome-shaped, promising a liberal and delicious filling. Wielding a large knife, Fluff cut into it and Hettie closed her eyes, waiting for the smell of meat juices to reach her nostrils. There was nothing, and she opened her eyes just in time to see a mass of green filling slide slowly away from the pastry as Fluff settled the first portion onto a plate and passed it to Tilly.

'I won't be offended if you just want to eat the pastry,' Fluff said, loading another plate and offering it to Hettie. 'We are overrun with courgettes at this time of year. Vegetables and the occasional bunch of flowers are the only payback I get from the allotments. To maintain their feudal rites to live and work on the land, my tenants have to offer some of the fruits of their labours – but all they grow is vegetables, flowers and the occasional strawberry patch. We did have a beekeeper up there at one time, but his bees turned on him for some reason, and that was the end of him *and* our honey supply. The bees had the decency to follow his coffin to the graveyard, but after the interment they took off towards Southwool and never returned. Blackberry took over his plot and she doesn't grow anything at all except scarecrows, so she makes up for it by helping me here at the Hall. She also delivers the more attractive, saleable produce to Malkin and Sprinkle's food hall, from where we receive a small but regular income. They call us the "Wither-Fork Hall Almost Organic" range.'

Hettie broke off a piece of pastry with her fork, and had to admit that it melted in the mouth. Tilly bravely tried a slice of courgette, discreetly removing it from her mouth almost immediately and placing it in her cardigan pocket to throw away later. She also pushed on with the pastry, and found it satisfying, if a little incomplete.

When the meal was over, Fluff Wither-Fork pushed the plates further down the table, keen not to be reminded of the unwanted courgettes that remained on everyone's plates. To commiserate – with herself as much as her guests – she announced brightly that it would be a cheese and potato pie tomorrow, then pulled her chair from the table and turned it to the fire, encouraging Hettie and Tilly to do the same.

'This body on the allotment is a damned nuisance,' she said, reminding Hettie and Tilly of the reason they were there. 'The Michaelmas Flower and Produce Show is this coming weekend, here in the grounds, and it quite simply has to go ahead. Apart from my garden tours, it's the one big paying event of the year, and without that revenue we won't survive the winter.'

'What *is* Michaelmas?' asked Tilly.

Fluff responded as if she had been asked to speak on her favourite subject. 'Well, the gist of it is that Michaelmas is on the twenty-ninth of September, and this year it falls on a Saturday. It's the day when all the taxes are collected by the landowners, when staff are hired at the big houses, when the harvest is secured for the winter, and any obligations are settled. In my case, there are no taxes to collect, I can't afford to hire any staff, and the harvest is non-existent because we haven't planted anything – except vegetables, of course. As far as obligations go, the ball is firmly in my court: I have to pay out for the upkeep of my tenants' housing and give them fifteen shillings per cat to spend as they wish. That is why the flower and produce show has to go ahead. If the town turns out in its usual numbers, I'll have enough money from the entrance fees to pay my tenants and keep the fires burning at the Hall during the winter.'

'None of that seems very fair,' observed Hettie. 'It's a strange sort of set-up where the landowner pays the tenants. How long has it been going on for?'

'About four hundred years, thanks to Lettuce Wither-Fork. She came to the Hall as a young bride, and – while her husband was hunting away from home – inadvertently set herself on fire in the church when a candle fell from one of the sconces. Luckily for her, the tenants were bringing in their produce for the harvest festival, which takes place the day before Michaelmas; they found her writhing before the altar, engulfed in flames, and quickly rolled her in the altar cloth so that she escaped with a light singeing. Her fur grew back in no time, judging by an old portrait I have of her in the west wing. The following day, she declared that all the tenants of Wither-Fork Hall should receive an annual sum of fifteen shillings, handed out on Michaelmas day for perpetuity, as a thank you for saving her life. Needless to say, according to the covenant she set up, any Wither-Fork heir who fails to execute her gift will be cursed.'

'It sounds to me like you're cursed already,' said Hettie, thinking aloud. 'Is there nothing you can do to break the covenant legally?'

Fluff shook her head. 'The only hope is to get some idiot to invest in the Hall, the land and the covenant. You only need to take a closer look at the state of the place to see that it's a money pit, even without the needs of the tenants. Then there's Mash, my sister. She has never been what I would call the brightest spark from the tinderbox. She and her ridiculous spouse have sitting-tenant rights on the gatehouse. Who's going to want to take all that on? Believe me, I've tried to offload the place. I even wrote a begging letter to the National Crust recently – they've been taking on land and setting up housing schemes for homeless cats, and I hoped this might be right up their street, but they didn't even have the decency to reply. It would appear that I can't even *give* it away.'

All three cats stared into the fireplace as the log smouldered and turned black, offering nothing by way of flames or heat. Hettie was beginning to realise that the least of Fluff Wither-Fork's worries was the body on the allotments, and the thought of raising the issue of a fee for her and Tilly to take on the case seemed almost too cruel – but there was rent to pay, and they had rather overspent on their holidays. She was about to break the silence when a voice came from behind.

'I know I'm late, but before you say anything it really isn't my fault. Micks spilt green slime all over the kitchen floor. He's been treading courgettes for the cauldron and they didn't work out, so he's decided on peas!'

There was no need for an introduction. Hettie, Tilly and Fluff turned as one to take in the vision of Mash Wither-Spoon, whose striking markings resembled her sister's. Her clothes were another story: she was swathed in black taffeta, tied at the middle with a rough length of binder twine. Fluff rose from the fire with a weary sigh, addressing the vision in black. 'And what – or who – are you supposed to be today, Mash?'

'I'm playing all three witches on the blasted heath, but I've been practising different voices to avoid confusion as there's only one of me.'

'Amen to that,' said Fluff, as Tilly stifled a giggle with her paw and Hettie marvelled at the landowner's calm acceptance of the situation.

Mash fumbled with her outfit and pulled out several letters. 'These arrived this morning for you – mostly junk, I think.'

Fluff took the letters and gave them a cursory glance. 'That's for me to decide,' she said, throwing them onto the dining-room table. 'All I ask is that you deliver them. I don't need a running commentary on the contents. Now, as you're here you can show my visitors back to the allotments, but before you go I need to talk to you about Micks.'

The smile that seemed to have planted itself on Mash Wither-Spoon's face disappeared. 'Why? What's he done now? You're always picking on him and spoiling his fun.'

'Look, Mash, I don't want to fall out with you, but there are times when Micks' idea of fun wears a little thin,' responded Fluff, trying to sound as reasonable as possible. 'As you live in the gatehouse, you are the first port of call for all visitors to the Hall. I don't expect my guests to be interrogated by Micks while he's wearing an assortment of ludicrous costumes and disguises. It simply won't do. Whatever games you feel the need to play in the privacy of your own four walls is up to you, but I don't want them extended to the day-to-day life of this estate. I thought we'd agreed that the gates should remain open during daylight hours? Which means that Micks – and you, for that matter – can keep yourselves to yourselves. I know it's radical, but perhaps Micks could busy himself with a little maintenance at the gatehouse if he finds himself with time on his paws, instead of marauding around like a one-cat amateur dramatic society.'

Mash lowered her head, and two large tears splashed onto the flagstone floor. 'But he loves opening the gates. He says it's the most important job he's ever done. He likes to pretend that Wither-Fork Hall and all the land belongs to him.'

'Well, it doesn't,' snapped Fluff, losing her patience and realising that Hettie and Tilly were awkward observers to family issues that didn't concern them. 'If he continues to interfere, I'll take the gate keys away from him and that will be that. Now, please take Miss Bagshot and her assistant back up to the allotments. I'm falling behind with the preparations for Saturday, and the marquee arrives tomorrow.'

Mash pulled a handkerchief out from under her costume and blew her nose. Nodding to Hettie and Tilly, she left the dining room. Fluff felt obliged to give an explanation. 'I do apologise,' she said, 'but these family matters are a constant demand on my time. We still haven't discussed your fee, or even confirmed that you're willing to investigate the matter at all. Perhaps you would join me for lunch tomorrow, here at the Hall, after you've had a chance to assess the situation fully? Then we can discuss terms and the way forward.'

Relieved that the subject of a fee had been broached, and more importantly that lunch would be a cheese and potato pie, Hettie agreed to Fluff's plan, and she and Tilly made their way through the entrance hall and out into the September drizzle, where Mash Wither-Spoon was waiting.

CHAPTER SIX

Their progress up the driveway was a silent one. Mash Wither-Spoon appeared to be deep in thought, and, on reaching the gatehouse, she left them without a word and let herself in by the back door, leaving them to make their own way up to the allotments. Hettie and Tilly reached the road in time to see the back of Shroud and Trestle's removal van disappearing down Wither-Fork Hill, with the corpse from Bonny Grubb's onion patch on board.

'Right,' said Hettie, tightening the belt on her mac. 'Let's see what this lot have to say for themselves. If we're efficient, we can get home before the Butters close up for the day. After that awful lunch, I think we'll need a couple of extra pies for supper with proper stuff inside them.'

'And some cream horns,' added Tilly, as they made their way down the allotment path, choosing to start at the bottom with Dahlia and Gladys Mulch.

The Mulch sisters had been driven into their shed by the drizzle, and Hettie and Tilly were welcomed inside to sit by their log burner. The small space was warm and cosy, and had all the trappings of a miniature house: a carpet on the floor; a small table by the window, boasting a vase of dahlias; and two dahlia-patterned fireside chairs, placed either side of the fire. A stew of sorts bubbled on top of the stove, sharing the hotplate with a kettle that had just begun to sing. The overall effect was one of blissful domesticity, and Hettie couldn't help but compare the starkness of Wither-Fork Hall with this tiny oasis of warmth and congeniality.

'Have you been here long?' Hettie asked, warming her paws on the stove and trying not to inhale the tempting smell of stew.

'We came just after the great storm,' said Dahlia. 'Took on poor Maud Clump's plot – her shed collapsed around her, God rest her soul.'

'Came just right for us, though,' chimed in Gladys. 'We'd just been turned out of the rectory after Pa died. There was no room for us when the new vicar moved in – the milk of feline kindness seemed to sour on her arrival.'

'We brought the dahlias with us,' continued her sister. 'I wasn't about to leave my namesakes behind. We went back to the rectory and dug them up at the dead of night as soon as we knew this plot was ours.'

'We had to wait three weeks after we'd applied, though,' added Gladys. 'Miss Wither-Fork said we'd have to fit the criteria, so we filled in her forms and waited for news.'

'And what were the criteria?'

Dahlia pulled a piece of paper from the table drawer. 'Here it is: "I bequeath plot five of the Wither-Fork lands to one or others who find they are without land in this parish and have no means to procure any, and they shall be served by my kin for as long as their need allows according to the covenant."' She folded the paper and put it back in the drawer. 'That comes from Lettuce Wither-Fork, whom the estate workers saved from burning hundreds of years ago. It means that my sister and I can stay here for as long as we like, and Miss Wither-Fork has to look after us on the condition that we send dahlias up to the Hall.'

Tilly had been quietly jotting notes down in her book, waiting for Hettie to get to the investigation. Knowing that the Butters' cream horns were always the first cakes to sell out, she gave her friend a gentle nudge to remind her of why they were there.

Hettie responded immediately. 'Are you both sure that you hadn't seen the dead cat on Bonny's allotment before?'

'Well, we don't see much down here at the bottom of the plots,' said Gladys. 'We see Clippy Lean coming and going from time to time, but we've fallen out with most of the others. Gertrude, who has the next plot, hasn't shared a word with us since last Michaelmas.'

'Is there any reason for that?'

'Earwigs,' replied Dahlia on her sister's behalf.

Hettie immediately wished she hadn't asked. 'They're very partial to dahlias,' Gladys continued, 'but – like the rest of us – they appreciate a change from time to time.'

'What do?'

'*Earwigs!*' the sisters chorused, and Tilly giggled as Gladys explained. 'They're happy in the dahlias we grow, but when we pick the flowers we give them a shake and the earwigs drop off and go and look for somewhere else to live. The trouble is, Gertrude Jingle grows prize white lilies, and some of our earwigs got onto her patch just before the Michaelmas Show last year and ate them. To make things even worse, we got best in show for our spiky dahlias and Gertrude had to settle for third prize with her white onions. As you can imagine, she wasn't best pleased.'

'And the earwigs seem to have spread to some of the other plots. Tarragon Trench says they've taken a liking to his catnip. He brings them back now and again, but you can't train an earwig, can you?' said Dahlia, shrugging her shoulders.

With another nudge in the back from Tilly, Hettie drew her conversation to a close, and the two cats stepped out of the little shed none the wiser than when they'd stepped in – except, perhaps, on the subject of earwigs.

CHAPTER SEVEN

'I think we'd better split up or we'll never get through this afternoon,' said Hettie. 'If you take a look round Clippy Lean's allotment, I'll take on Gertrude Jingle.'

'What are we looking for?' asked Tilly, poised for instructions.

'I've no idea until we find it, but I don't believe for a minute that this murder took place without anyone up here noticing something.'

'Especially the murderer,' said Tilly sagely, opening the gate to Clippy Lean's plot.

Hettie moved next door from the Mulch sisters and stood watching while the cat identified in Jeremiah Corbit's line-up as Gertrude Jingle pottered about.

She seemed oblivious to anything but the flowers she nurtured, and not even the drizzle could distract her as she tended a bed of giant lilies. She wore a wide-brimmed hat, tied with a sash under her chin, and what looked like a heavily embroidered dressing gown; the dressing gown reached down to the ground, and made the heavy garden boots that peeped out from under it look more than a little out of place. The cat was totally at one with her flowers as she wielded a pair of clippers, removing a lily here and there, and seeming to thank the plant as she deadheaded it. She placed the old flower heads in a trug, which swung from one of her paws, and worked her way slowly and methodically along the row.

Hettie felt bad about disturbing such a tranquil scene, but there was a job to be done. 'Miss Jingle?' she said, opening the gate. 'May I have a word with you?'

The cat turned and blinked at Hettie. 'You'll have to speak up,' she shouted. 'I'm not used to conversation. I find conversing with my flowers so much easier now my hearing's gone. Are you here to talk about that business on Bonny Grubb's plot?'

Hettie shut the gate behind her and moved closer to make the interview less of a shouting match. 'Yes, that's right. I just wanted to know if you've noticed anything out of the ordinary lately?'

The cat put her trug down and waved her paw around. 'Out of the ordinary, you say? Well, just open your eyes. What do you see?'

Hettie looked round, a little bewildered. 'Er, lots of lovely flowers,' she shouted.

'Not just any flowers. Look again,' said the cat, getting agitated.

Hettie did as she was told and surveyed the plot once more. This time, the penny dropped. 'They're all white?'

'Bravo! And in answer to your question, they are *all* out of the ordinary. My flowers represent purity and innocence, honesty and perfection. They are free from sin. They illuminate and inspire.' With that, she took off for a grand tour of the allotment, shouting out the names as she went. 'Gardenia, cape jasmine, *Helleborus niger*, *Viburnum opulus*, *Euonymus japonicus*, *Lilium candidum* – and here are my prize orientals, Stargazer. See their crimson centres? Lethal and beautiful to the same degree.'

'Why are they lethal?' Hettie enquired, trying to sound interested.

'Stamens and pollen, all poisonous. You should talk to Micks Wither-Spoon.'

'About poisons?' Hettie was more confused than ever.

Gertrude Jingle looked as bewildered as Hettie felt. 'Why would you want to talk to Micks about poisons? He's half-witted at the best of times. You couldn't trust him with poisons. He'd end up stirring it into his tea, or someone else's by mistake.'

The cat chuckled to herself and Hettie tried once more. 'So what *should* I talk to Micks Wither-Spoon about?'

'Living in an ivory tower,' she said, waving her paw in the direction of the gatehouse. 'He doesn't miss a thing from up there. Hapless boy, really – inhabits his own dramas, and just look at those Japanese anemones.'

Hettie watched as Gertrude Jingle returned to her flowers, shouting out their names as if she were calling out the register in a schoolroom. She realised that she was getting nowhere fast with the investigation, and was coming to the conclusion that Lettuce Wither-Fork should have added barking mad to her criteria. She left Miss Jingle to her white flowers and went off to find Tilly, casting an eye in the direction of the gatehouse just in time to see Micks Wither-Spoon disappearing from his turret.

'How did you get on with Miss Jingle?' asked Tilly as she emerged from Clippy Lean's shed, brushing the dust off her paws.

'Don't even ask, but I doubt that she's murdered anybody. In a world of her own, that one, as long as it's white. She did point out that Micks Wither-Spoon might be worth talking to as he has a good vantage point from his battlements, but I'm not sure I can face that today.'

Tilly could see that Hettie's encounter with Gertrude Jingle had not advanced the case in any way, and she'd found nothing of interest on Clippy Lean's plot, either. The town's bus conductress was clearly a grower of very fine vegetables, and Tilly had marvelled at the leeks, peas and beans; the rhubarb was taller than she was, with giant, red-veined leaves that created a canopy of shade that would be perfect to snooze under on a hot sunny day. The only unexpected item was in Clippy's shed – a bus seat in red leather, clearly rescued from an out-of-service vehicle and given a loving home amid the gardening necessities. 'What's next?' she asked, shutting Clippy's gate behind her.

'I'd like to say home, a pie, a cream horn and a fire,' grumbled Hettie, 'but it's not going to happen until we've had a word with the rest of them up here. Let's try this lot.' She eyed up the next gate along the path and noted that it was made from a ship's wheel; the nautical theme continued with a large upturned boat, which had a chimney sticking out of the top and a series of round windows dotted along the hull.

'Ooh, that's lovely,' said Tilly in admiration, as the door in the centre of the boat opened to reveal Rooster Chit.

'Welcome to our patch, my dears, and come in out of this rain. Desiree 'as just snatched a batch of potato cakes from 'er oven.' He spoke with a mild West Country accent that Tilly found instantly attractive, and his words were made all the more inviting by the smell of baking, which escaped from the door as Rooster threw it wide open.

At the promise of food, Hettie bustled forward in a

rather ungainly manner and flattened Rooster against the door on her way into the Chits' boathouse. Inside, the scene was one of perfect peace and tranquillity, and Tilly held her breath as she took in every detail of the little house – the high-domed ceiling with bunks cut into its sides, the walls hung with ropes and coloured glass balls, which twinkled in the lantern light, giving everything a soft, warm glow. There were stars and a moon painted in silver on the roof boards, and the furniture below – tiny lockers and a dresser full of plates and cups – was built into the walls. A central table and benches had been bolted to the floor, and at the far end a galley kitchen with a range dominated a good third of the space. On either side of the stove, rows of shelving were stacked with supplies: bags of flour; sugar; and glass jars of nuts, currants and jams. Above the range, a row of copper pans and utensils sparkled.

Queen of her domain, like a figurehead from an old tall ship, Desiree Chit was in full sail by her stove, transferring a baking tray full of golden potato cakes onto a plate. 'Come in, come in, an' leave that drizzle at the door, my dears,' she said as she banged the cakes down on the table. 'Get your paws round one of these.'

Hettie didn't wait for a second invitation and slid onto the nearest bench, grasping a cake in both paws and burning her mouth as she bit into the buttery treat. 'These are delicious, Mrs Chit,' she said through a mouthful of hot potato.

'That's why I 'auled 'er ashore and made an 'onest cat of 'er. No one cooks potatoes like my darlin' Desiree.'

'Hush your nonsense, Rooster Chit! Make yourself useful and fill some glasses with your nice cordial – that'll go lovely with me cakes.'

Rooster did as he was told and Desiree sat her substantial form down next to Tilly, who was still staring in wonderment around the boathouse, cautiously nibbling on a cake and trying not to burn her mouth. 'You look like you need feedin' up, my dear,' she said, giving Tilly a half-hug. 'More potato, less meat – that's the way to put flesh on your bones.'

Rooster returned to the table with four glasses full of a pink liquid and Hettie accepted one gratefully, hoping that it would alleviate the burning sensation in her mouth. The drink did calm things down for a moment or two, but then Hettie's head began to swim as the liquid took effect. Noticing her distress, Rooster came to the rescue with a glass of water. 'You 'ave to build up a tolerance to my cordial, see. You'll be as right as a ship's compass in a minute or two. 'Ave another cake to 'elp it down.'

Tilly watched as her friend recovered, helped by another potato cake and several more sips of water. Having seen Hettie's reaction, she decided to give the cordial a miss, which was just as well as Desiree had absent-mindedly downed it along with her own. A high-pitched screeching sound suddenly filled the air and all eyes turned to one of the bunks, where a small, furry, striped face appeared, blinking down at them. Desiree responded immediately. 'Come on, my little dear. No need for all of that. We got visitors, so you come down an' 'ave one of these nice cakes.' Desiree lifted the kitten down from the bunk and placed him on the table. Breaking a cake in half, she put a piece in his paws. 'My poor little Blight's got himself upset by that cat on Bonny's patch. It took me ages to settle 'im for 'is afternoon nap. 'E's a sensitive little mite.'

The mention of the situation on Bonny Grubb's allotment reminded Hettie that there was work to be done, even though her investigation was turning into a rather fine tea party. Brushing the crumbs from the front of her mac and taking another sip of water, she began her questioning, addressing the senior Chits while Tilly positioned herself again with her notepad and pencil. 'I'm sorry to have caused distress earlier by asking you to view the body,' Hettie began, 'but I was hoping that someone would recognise him. Are you both sure you haven't seen him before? I realise he may have looked quite different when he was alive.'

Blight Chit let out another wail and this time it was Rooster who attended the kitten. He lifted him off the table and settled him on a rug by the stove, giving him a large piece of paper and a pot of paint from one of the shelves. Hettie and Tilly watched as Rooster pulled a large potato from a basket by the range and began to cut into it with a knife. Blight screeched with delight as his father dipped the potato into the paint and dabbed it onto the top corner of the paper, leaving a pattern, which Blight – now in possession of the potato – proceeded to repeat across the paper, purring and chirruping loudly.

Rooster returned to the table to answer Hettie's question. 'We gets all sorts up 'ere, and it's 'ard to say who you know and who you don't – but by 'is clothes, 'e's not typical. Struck me as a posh cat from a big city. Out of place, really. More Miss Wither-Fork's sort of cat – gentry, like.'

'He could be one of Micks' and Mash's cronies,' added Desiree. 'Them Wither-Spoons are a funny lot. The shame of it is that Mash is turning into one. She's no 'elp to her poor sister, who has the cares of the world 'eaped upon her.'

Hettie liked the Chits and was keen to learn more about them, even if it had no bearing on the case. 'How long have you been resident on the allotments?' she asked, as Desiree proffered another potato cake in her direction.

'Well now, it must be ten years since I left the sea. A nasty accident with a shoal of 'addock did for me, and we lost our onshore cottage as it came with the job,' Rooster explained. 'We moved shortly after that, and we were 'ere for the great storm. We lost more than a few potatoes that night, didn't we, my dear?' He patted Desiree's paw as an extreme sadness spread across her face. 'Our three lovely kittens, all blown from their beds. We found 'em in a ditch at the bottom of Wither-Fork Hill early the next morning. Miss Wither-Fork was so kind – she let us bury 'em on our patch. Desiree's made a lovely garden for 'em. That's why I 'ad my old boat brought up 'ere to make us a home. We'll never leave with our family around us, and young Blight lets the sun in on sad days. 'E was an unexpected joy to us both.'

Hettie put down the remains of her cake, feeling that she'd intruded into a part of the Chits' lives that was still unbearably raw. Tilly felt their sadness, too, and squeezed Desiree's paw in an act of solidarity. As if on cue, Blight scrambled up onto the table and presented Desiree with his paint-spattered artwork, the potato patterns indistinct but just about recognisable. All sadness was dispelled as the kitten's proud parents looked at the shambolic mess of wet paint and soggy paper. Desiree rose from the table and pinned the picture to the wall by the range, where it joined a gallery of similar efforts. She returned to the table with a damp cloth, and – under mild protestations – cleaned the paint from the kitten's paws, face and ears.

Hettie felt that it was a good moment to take their leave and signalled to Tilly, who put her notepad and pencil back into her mac pocket. 'Thank you for the lovely cakes and cordial,' she said as she tightened her belt on a full stomach. 'May we call on you again if we need to?'

'You'll always find a welcome 'ere,' said Rooster. 'Let's 'ope for calmer seas next time you visit. No point in showin' you round the allotment in this drizzle. I 'ope it clears tomorrow, as I've got to lift me best spuds for the show. Clippy's grown a good crop this year, and old misery guts up the row's been braggin' about the size of his Maris Pipers, so I got a bit of competition on me paws.'

'Misery guts?' said Hettie, stepping out into the rain.

'Jeremiah Corbit,' said Rooster, pointing in the direction of the next allotment. ''E thinks 'e runs things round 'ere, but the fact is 'e don't. I know 'e manages to put up a few 'ackles, but the secret's not to rise to the bait. That way, you can swim in your own pond 'appily.'

On that note, Hettie and Tilly said their goodbyes and all three Chits waved them off from their boathouse door.

CHAPTER EIGHT

Jeremiah Corbit was waiting at his gate as Hettie and Tilly approached. He was puffing on a rather unpleasant-smelling clay pipe, blowing the acrid smoke out onto the path. Hettie waved the smoke away with her paw and Corbit renewed the insult by blowing another plume into her face. 'I can see you're one of those reformed smokers,' he said. 'Typical attitude of the middle classes – taking a dim view of the workers and their simple pleasures.'

'I'm sorry,' said Hettie, feeling her hackles begin to rise. 'I'm not sure what you mean. I do actually enjoy a pipe of my own and have no particular views on workers or the middle classes. I'm here to investigate a murder, that's all.'

Tilly had been hiding behind Hettie, having taken an instant dislike to the cat. She emerged slowly to take her place by Hettie's side. Jeremiah stared down at her for a second before offering another assessment. 'Two females calling yourselves detectives, poking your snouts into lives that don't concern you; why aren't you at home knitting jumpers and making curtains or something?'

Hettie rose to the bait against Rooster Chit's advice. 'Ah well, you see, Mr Corbit, we only knit and sew in the evenings, which leaves our days free for gainful employment. We do our washing, ironing and cooking before we start our day's work, because we female cats are multi-skilled and able to turn our paws to anything, including running a rather successful detective agency. I believe you excel in compost?'

Tilly did her best to suppress a giggle, disguising it with a loud cough. Temporarily thrown off balance, Jeremiah Corbit opened the gate to let them through to his allotment. At first sight, it was a bleak, inhospitable patch of land. Most of the ground was taken up with giant stacks of rotting vegetables and other garden detritus; even though the rain was now falling steadily, the heaps steamed and fermented, giving off the vilest of smells and making Corbit's pipe tobacco almost sweet by comparison. At the end of the allotment stood a ramshackle shed, made of various bits of wood, metal and felting; to the side of the shed, there was a row of giant water butts and a small cultivated patch of potatoes, fenced off by bits of coiled barbed wire.

'I would ask you in out of the rain, but there doesn't seem much point. I've nothing to say to you, and it's no surprise to me that the Bonny Grubbs of this world spend their time disrupting an orderly existence. Gypsies, living off the fat of the land, sucking up to the aristocats, taking up homes that working cats need – and now a body turns up on her patch and we're all turned into murder suspects overnight.'

The rain was trickling down Hettie's neck as she listened to the venom coming from Corbit's mouth, but she found herself quite fascinated by his views on Bonny Grubb and prompted him to give a verdict on some of the other residents. 'Well, I can see very clearly that you are a cat of the world,' she said, turning on the famous Bagshot charm. 'You obviously hold strong and considered views beyond the intelligence of those who live up here on the allotments, which makes you exactly the cat I need to help with my enquiries. Tell me about the other tenants.'

Hettie had scored the perfect goal. Corbit turned on his heel and led them down the plot to his shed, out of the rain. He proffered a bench covered with sacking just inside the door, then settled on a grubbily covered bed, knocking his pipe out on the edge of it. The inside of the shed was no less ramshackle than the outside, offering a spartan existence with hardly any comfort at all. The walls were dark and smelt of creosote, and the only hint of life was in a collection of webs that hung from the ceiling; Tilly watched for some time as several large black harvest spiders went about their business, stitching flies and other small insects into their woven nests. An old paraffin lamp stood redundant in the corner, offering only the slightest promise of heat on a winter's night. The overall effect was of a desperate existence.

The shed reminded Tilly of her homeless days, clinging to the library's radiators for warmth by day before being turned out to wander the cold, frosty streets in search of a night-time shelter. In those far-off days, old sheds had been her salvation – but she had had no choice; looking round Jeremiah Corbit's apology for a home, she couldn't help but think that this frugal life was one that he'd chosen. She would have given both her front paws for a plot of land on those dark cold nights, when to stay awake was to stay alive. She shivered, as much from the memory as the rain, and pulled a soggy notepad out of her mac pocket as Hettie engaged Jeremiah Corbit on the finer points of his allotment colleagues.

'Most of them shouldn't be up here at all,' Corbit began. 'Take the Mulch sisters – middle-class vicar's daughters, more used to patronising the poor of the parish with their polite manners and empty gestures. Just because they were turned out of the rectory, doesn't give them the right to live up here.' Hettie was about to point out that they *had* been made homeless, which fitted the criteria of Lettuce Wither-Fork's covenant, but decided to hold her tongue while he was in full flow. 'And as for the ridiculous Miss Jingle – upper-class spinster dancing round her plot like some demented fairy. Those lily bulbs don't come cheap, and they say she's got pots of money under her feather mattress. She grows nothing for the good of society, and flowers are an indulgence we can't afford with so many cats out there starving. The only reason she's got that plot is because Miss Wither-Fork was tricked into thinking she was old and destitute. Shame the workhouses have closed – a spell in there would buck her ideas up.'

'And the Chits?' Hettie said, bracing herself for more of Corbit's uncharitable thoughts.

'Well, they're almost the exception. He's a worker, of sorts, and he had a family to support after he lost his job. I've no real gripe with them, and he does supply me with a good deal of potato tops for composting. That kitten screeches a lot, but they do keep themselves to themselves, and they do lend a paw in a crisis. Blackberry Tibbs is another one whose face doesn't fit. She spends most of her time up at the Hall when she's not making those stupid scarecrows. I hear her talking to them sometimes when I'm aerating my heaps. No spreading of wealth there – she gets a tidy sum from selling those straw dolls on sticks, and she's wheedled her way in up at Wither-Fork Hall as a maid of all work. Hardly a cat in need.'

'You haven't mentioned the two non-resident plots,' said Hettie, and Tilly turned to a clean page in her notebook, wondering when they would get to the murder.

'That's because they *are* non-resident,' said Corbit. 'They're probably the worst of the lot, just wanting an extra bit of garden to grow some vegetables. The Gamp sisters have one of those oh-so-nice little bungalows in Sheba Gardens, full of home comforts, and have you seen their allotment?'

Hettie shook her head, and Corbit continued, 'Well, I won't spoil it for you. Let's just say that having an allotment is a novelty for them. They waste most of what they grow. Clippy Lean has a flat in the town without a garden, so she treats her allotment as a hobby and pops up here whenever she feels like it, abandoning her passengers at the bottom of Wither-Fork Hill. It's an outrage – just because she sells the tickets on the gate at the Michaelmas Show, she thinks she can get away with murder.'

Hettie couldn't help but raise an eyebrow at Corbit's last comment, suddenly remembering why she was there. Although Tarragon Trench and Apple Chutney hadn't been mentioned so far, she was keen to move things on, but couldn't resist enquiring as to how Jeremiah himself had qualified for an allotment.

'And what brought you to this?' she asked innocently, looking up as a giant spider made steady progress across the roof of the shed before dropping down onto Jeremiah's bed. In one fast movement, he squashed it with his paw.

'I worked at the old fish canning factory in Southwool. After a while, the cats elected me as their representative to the management. It was a good job, and I settled down with one of the canners from the shop floor – sweet little thing, she was. We set up home together and then the trouble started. The managers started to lay cats off as they brought in new machinery, and in the end all our jobs were at risk. I called the workers together, and we locked ourselves into the factory for two weeks and smashed up all the new machines. While I was held up with the workers, I found out that my dear little fish canner had taken up with one of the managers. I admit, it threw me into a rage, and I set fire to the factory with us all inside. Most cats escaped with minor burns, but they all turned on me and hung me out to dry. I was forced to walk away with no home, no job and nothing in my pocket – and what's worse, no thanks for standing up for workers' rights. Reluctantly, I applied to Miss Wither-Fork the week after the great storm, and I've been here ever since, living like a pauper on a rich cat's land. Another triumph for the upper classes,' he finished bitterly.

Hettie tried hard but could find no sympathy for him. From what she'd seen so far, all the residents had attempted to make the best of things and all seemed content with their lot; Corbit had merely continued to ruffle feathers and question the way that other cats lived their lives, maintaining a high opinion of himself along the way. It was Fluff Wither-Fork who should be congratulated for offering shelter and land to so many of society's oddities, and at such great cost to herself.

Tilly shivered and Hettie decided that they had both had enough of the Wither-Fork allotments for one day. They were soaked to the skin and in desperate need of their own fireside and a Butters' supper. Tarragon Trench and Apple Chutney would have to wait, along with the Gamp sisters and Blackberry Tibbs. The two cats took their leave of Jeremiah Corbit and made tracks for the main road. There was no sign of Clippy Lean's bus so they set off at a brisk pace down Wither-Fork Hill, relieved that the rain had settled back into a harmless, fine drizzle.

CHAPTER NINE

An hour later, they fell over the threshold of Betty and Beryl Butter's pie and pastry shop. The sisters were wiping down their surfaces, and to Hettie's horror there was no sign of a pie or pastry to be had. Betty could see the distress on her face, and noticed the dishevelled state of both her lodgers. 'Ee, whatever have you two been up to? Come and look at them, sister,' she said, as Beryl bustled out of the window with a J cloth full of crumbs in her paw.

'My, my – what a state to get in. It's just as well we put your dinners to one side, isn't it, sister?'

Hettie's and Tilly's hearts leapt in unison as Betty retrieved a large paper bag from behind the counter.

'Two steak and kidney, two cream horns, and a stray bit of flapjack. How's that for extrasensory confection? Now, get yourselves into your room before you catch your deaths.'

Hettie and Tilly did as they were told. The Lancashire sisters were the closest thing either of them had to a mother, and their kindness and protection had seen the friends through several rough patches since they moved into the old storeroom at the back of the bakery. They peeled their wet macs off immediately, and Tilly leapt to the hearth to lay a fire; within minutes, the flames began to climb up the chimney breast as she added more coal. Hettie retrieved Tilly's pyjamas and her own dressing gown from the filing cabinet, while Tilly switched on the TV in time for the six o'clock news. Happy to be cosy and dry at last, the two cats sat by the fire, warming their paws, and Hettie was relieved that the news carried nothing on the allotment murder: the last thing they or Fluff Wither-Fork needed at this point was a media storm. It was only a matter of time before the dead cat would be missed, but by then Hettie hoped to have identified the killer.

After the 'and finally', a weather cat announced that from tomorrow there was going to be an Indian summer, which would last for at least five days – good news for their investigations and for the event preparations up at Wither-Fork Hall. 'What shall we do next?' said Tilly. 'Supper or a catch-up on the case?'

'I'm hungry but not desperate, so let's get the work out of the way first. I don't think we've much to go on, but we need to take a close look at the notebook that Bonny removed from the body. Alfred Hitchcat's *Psycho* is on later. We could have a late supper and watch that.'

Tilly clapped her paws at the prospect of a scary film and a late supper, and retrieved the notebook from her mac pocket, settling down with it on her blanket by the fire. Hettie filled her catnip pipe and puffed out a line of smoke rings, waiting for Tilly to report her findings. 'Well, there's definitely no name or address,' she began. 'Looking closer, it's more of a sketchbook. There are some lovely drawings of lakes and trees and farmland, with little villages and big houses. This one looks a bit like Wither-Fork Hall. There are some scribbly notes about acres and sea levels on some of the sketches, and several pages at the back on different sorts of trees. The drawings are really very good. I think he must have been some sort of artist. Maybe he was on a sketching holiday.'

Hettie flicked through several of the pages that Tilly had drawn her attention to. 'He wasn't dressed for a sketching holiday, that much we do know. And why would he be up on the allotments? He obviously died where he was attacked, because there was no sign of the body having been dumped there. Let's go back over what we've learnt today.'

Tilly obliged by reaching for her own notepad, slowly drying out by the fire. 'I've called my notes "The Michaelmas Murder" because Michaelmas is such a lovely word,' she said, and Hettie nodded her approval, marvelling at the way in which Tilly found something positive in the darkest of subjects; her sunny disposition kept them both going at times. 'I've jotted down the details of the body first,' Tilly continued, squinting at her own scribble. 'I've got posh coat and boots, bashed in head with rock, lots of blood all over onions, notebook and coins in pockets. There's a list of all the cats with allotments next. Is it too early to do a suspect list?'

Hettie thought for a moment. 'Let's leave that until last, and go through what we know.'

'Well, I've made a note of Bonny Grubb first. She says she saw or heard nothing because she was out for the count on moonshine, but she did go through his pockets and didn't own up straight away, so I suppose that's a black mark against her. I've also noted that Blackberry Tibbs hasn't seen the body because she was up at the Hall cooking that awful pie.' At the recollection of lunch, Tilly jumped up from her blanket and retrieved a ball of soggy courgette from her cardigan pocket, then threw it into the fire where it sizzled and died. Resuming her report, Tilly continued, 'I've got a bit on Fluff Wither-Fork next – cash poor, house falling down, stuck with Lettuce Wither-Fork's legacy and Micks and Mash Wither-Spoon.'

Hettie laughed. 'I couldn't have put it better myself. Add the Michaelmas Flower and Produce Show to that – it connects the allotments to the Hall, and Fluff was very concerned that the murder would put paid to her show and the income from it. As a long shot, someone might be trying to sabotage the show – it's something to consider, at least. There *does* seem to be a competitive spirit regarding vegetables on the allotments – and flowers, for that matter – but murder seems a little extreme.'

Tilly added to her notes and turned the page. 'Dahlia and Gladys Mulch next. Turned out of rectory, fit criteria – although I'm not sure how to spell it – dug up dahlias, trouble with earwigs and Gertrude Jingle. Nothing really to report on Clippy Lean's patch, except a bus seat in her shed. I've written Gertrude Jingle down – is there anything you want me to say about her?'

'Barking mad would be fairly accurate, but she did point out that Micks Wither-Spoon had a good vantage point over the allotments from one of his gatehouse turrets, so we need to pay him a call tomorrow, heaven help us. She did mutter something about poison and lilies as well, but I think that was part of her horticultural ramblings. Let's move on to the Chits.'

In Tilly's notebook, Rooster and Desiree Chit had a whole page to themselves, mainly because

Tilly was so taken with their beautiful boathouse that she'd written detailed notes on their furniture and decorations, even though they had nothing to do with the case. She decided to skip all the lovely descriptive bits and cut to the chase, as supper awaited and it was only half an hour before the film started. 'Rooster said that the dead cat might be one of Micks Wither-Spoon's cronies, and that all sorts of cats came and went up on the allotments. He agrees with us that the victim probably came from a big city. He also called Jeremiah Corbit a misery guts and was worried about lifting his potatoes for the show. I've made a note about them losing three kittens in the great storm because that was very sad.'

Hettie agreed and began to eye up the paper bag containing their supper. 'Just Corbit to go, then, and he's probably the most interesting so far. He's got a real axe to grind, if you ask me – what have you got on him?'

'I've started with not very nice and a bit of a bully,' said Tilly. 'Chauvinist – not sure how to spell that – horrid compost heaps, nasty little shed with spiders, troublemaker, nasty about the other cats, seemed to think they had no right to the allotments, not very nice about Fluff Wither-Fork, caused canning factory fire in Southwool.'

'In short,' said Hettie, 'just as Rooster Chit said – a misery guts. I wonder if any cats died in that fire?

78

Maybe someone traced him to the allotments looking for revenge and got more than they bargained for. Make a note to check that out – a quick call to Hacky Redtop at the local paper should give us an answer. Let's make a list of suspects, then we can get on with our evening. It's been a long day.'

Tilly selected a clean page and wrote 'suspects' at the top of it. 'Shall I put Jeremiah Corbit first, as we don't like him much?'

'Yes, I think that's an excellent idea. Put the Mulch sisters next – they might be capable of murder. We know very little so far about Blackberry Tibbs, but she does come and go a lot between the Hall and her allotment, so stick her down, followed by Micks and Mash Wither-Spoon. I think we should speak to them first tomorrow morning. If Micks has a grandstand view of the allotments, he may have seen something, and his name *has* come up a couple of times in conversation.'

'What about Gertrude Jingle and the Chits? And then there's Bonny Grubb, and Fluff Wither-Fork herself.'

Hettie considered for a moment. 'I doubt that any of them would be capable of bashing a cat's head in. Bonny is a thief and a twister of the truth, but she's no killer. The Chits have had too much sorrow to court any more. Gertrude Jingle's world doesn't exist beyond her own allotment, and as for Fluff

Wither-Fork . . .' Hettie paused, weighing up the probabilities. 'Oh, put them all on the list and let's see what tomorrow brings. Now, break out the pies. We've got five minutes before the film starts.'

The supper and the film went down very well, although Tilly made a mental note that if she and Hettie could ever afford a shower they wouldn't bother with the curtain. She fell into a deep sleep, dreaming of cats in rocking chairs being slashed to death on the Wither-Fork allotments. The morning would confirm that the dream had been a premonition of sorts, with one name erased from her list of suspects.

CHAPTER TEN

As the weather cat had promised, Hettie and Tilly awoke to bright sunshine and a cloudless sky. With an uncharacteristic spring in their step, the two cats rose early and exchanged their luncheon vouchers for Betty's sausage, liver and bacon pies, and two of Beryl's custard tarts. With supper secured, they strode purposefully out to await the arrival of Clippy Lean's bus.

The town's high street was already a hive of activity, with cats out shopping or gathered in clumps, putting the world to rights. Lavender Stamp, the postmistress, was sweeping the pavement outside, much to the annoyance of the queue that was building at her counter. Her queues were legendary, as Lavender believed that anything that her post office dispensed was worth waiting for, and her shop frontage was as important to her as the many cats who needed stamps, postal orders and a variety of long-winded official forms. Lavender liked to be in control, and keeping her customers waiting – knowing that she was the only post office in town – made her day. Every day.

A bus stop outside the post office was convenient for most cats, but for those waiting there when Lavender was in full flight with her yard brush, things could – and often did – get nasty. Hettie and Tilly had an ambivalent relationship with the postmistress, and they had clashed on several occasions; this morning it seemed that Lavender was in one of her more spiteful moods, apparently needing to sweep the exact bit of pavement on which they were standing. Tilly obliged and moved out of the way as the broom approached, but Hettie stood firm, maintaining her stronghold on the pavement as the brush came to an abrupt stop at the back of her heels. Lavender pushed harder, and Hettie remained stubbornly glued to the spot. The queue inside spilt out onto the pavement, turning into enthusiastic spectators as a battle of wills unfolded before them. Tilly, who avoided confrontation whenever she could, spotted a heap of sticky chewing gum on the pavement, close to Lavender's bright-red postbox, and decided to use it as a diplomatic way of defusing the situation. 'Miss Stamp, some horrid cat has spat their gum out in front of your box,' she said. 'That's going to stick to everyone who tries to post a letter if it's not removed.' The distraction worked. Lavender retreated back into the post office and returned minutes later with a kettle of boiling water and a paint scraper, just as Clippy Lean's bus loomed into view.

Hettie and Tilly made their way up to the top deck to sit at the front, where they were soon joined by Clippy. Instead of dispensing their tickets, she waved Tilly's paw of change away and sat down next to them. 'No charge today,' she said. 'I just wondered how it was all going?'

Hettie, still irritated by her encounter with Lavender Stamp, was tempted to reply 'How is all *what* going?', but she knew by the enthusiasm of the question that Clippy was angling for an update on the case and decided to ask a few questions of her own as the bus ambled through the town. 'Not very well at the moment, Clippy,' she began. 'We still have to talk to a few more of the residents, but nobody so far has any idea who the dead cat could be. Do you get on well with the others on the allotment?'

'Most of them,' said Clippy, making herself comfortable. 'The Mulch sisters are lovely, and I love Miss Jingle – she's so interesting with her white flowers. I fetch her shopping sometimes – she doesn't like to leave her patch because she's afraid someone will take it off her. She gets quite upset about it sometimes. I think she married into the high life because she's come from a great big house with servants and everything, but her nephew gambled the lot away after she was widowed. It broke her heart to be made homeless. She had to leave her beautiful gardens behind, and her flowers are all she has left.'

'Why does she think she might lose her allotment?' asked Tilly, intrigued to learn more.

'Mostly because Jeremiah says she shouldn't be there in the first place, and she's frightened of him. Come to think of it, he doesn't like any of us being up there, except himself of course. I steer clear of him and keep my compost to myself. He saw my uncle Bobby out of a job when he burnt the old canning factory down in Southwool. He was supposed to be standing up for workers' rights, but most of them were so badly burnt that they'll never work again.'

The bus came to a standstill and several passengers got on. Clippy swung herself down the stairs to issue tickets to the newcomers, then returned to Hettie and Tilly. Realising that the interruptions would continue, Hettie decided to ask about the next interviewee on her list. 'What about Micks Wither-Spoon? Miss Jingle says he watches the allotments from the gatehouse.'

Clippy smiled. 'Dear old Micks, bless him. He likes to show an interest, especially since Mash bought him some binoculars for his birthday. There's no side to him at all – he just plays his games all the day long. Mash does her best with him, but he's a bit of a Peter Pan – never really grew up, and she's almost as bad. They drive Miss Wither-Fork up the wall sometimes. I feel sorry for her, really, stuck in that crumbling mansion. According to Blackberry, she can't even afford heating, but there's no shortage of home comforts at the gatehouse – snug as bugs in rugs.'

Clippy stood up briefly to ring the bell as two cats showed signs of wanting to get off. The bus driver responded by slamming on his brakes and opening the folding doors in one movement; the stop was an unscheduled one, but the grateful passengers waved their thanks and the bus lurched on its way again. Hettie stared out of the window, realising that they were fast approaching Wither-Fork Hill, where their illuminating conversation with the town's award-winning bus conductress would come to an end. 'Just one last question, Clippy. We haven't talked to Tarragon Trench or Apple Chutney yet – what are they like?'

'Well, I think you'll find Tarragon a bit strange at first. He's rather too fond of catnip and never quite with us, if you know what I mean. Not a recreational smoker, more a way of life. He's a bit of a hippy, really – peace and love and all that stuff from the sixties. Apple's a lovely cat. Her real name is Apple Smith, but she loves making her chutneys so much that she's changed her name to go with them. The only thing is, she hates having her plot next to Jeremiah because of his horrid compost heaps – and he's put barbed wire up on his boundary, which isn't very friendly. She's asked Miss Wither-Fork if she can move to another plot when one comes up. Now, hold on and keep everything crossed – we're at the bottom of the hill!'

Hettie, Tilly, Clippy and the rest of the passengers all leant forward in their seats as if willing the bus to climb the hill; this time, the engine roared as the driver forced the bus into low gear, pushing his paw down hard on the accelerator as the bus slowly but surely climbed to the summit. There was rapturous applause and cheering from all the cats on board, and Clippy took a bow on behalf of the bus and the driver. She waved Hettie and Tilly off as they made their way to the gatehouse, hoping to find Micks Wither-Spoon at home.

As instructed, the gates to Wither-Fork Hall were open, and Hettie could see a great deal of activity taking place in the parkland beyond: three large marquees and a series of tents lay on the grass, waiting to be erected, and several cats stood round scratching their heads and directing each other. A number of vendors' caravans were also setting up to offer light refreshments to the hoards who would descend at the weekend. By contrast, the gatehouse looked uninhabited: there was no sign of Micks on his battlements, and as Hettie and Tilly made their way round to the back door, they noticed that the curtains were drawn in what they took to be the kitchen. Hettie knocked on the door and waited but there was no reply, only a strange murmuring sound coming from within.

Tilly noticed a small chink in the kitchen curtains and climbed up on a couple of well-placed logs to see if she could see through the window. 'There's definitely something going on in there,' she reported as the logs gave way and she banged her chin on the windowsill. 'It's all green and swirly, like under the sea.'

Tilly's assessment of what was going on in the Wither-Spoons' kitchen turned out to be more accurate than it sounded. After several more bangs on the door, it was finally opened by Micks, wearing chain mail over a dress and with a cardboard crown perched on his head. 'Splendid!' he said. 'An audience – just what we need. Come in and perch yourselves on the edge of the blasted heath.'

Hettie was somewhat taken aback by their welcome, but twice as shocked by the vision that greeted them as they stepped inside the kitchen. What she assumed to be Mash Wither-Spoon was dancing round a bubbling, volcanic cauldron, which exuded something that looked like pea soup. Mash had enhanced the outfit from the day before with a headband of dangling, slimy seaweed, topping everything off with a battered witch's hat for extra effect. The whole scene was bathed in a green light, created by makeshift lamps draped in green crêpe paper. As Tilly had quite rightly suggested, the overall effect looked like something from *Voyage to the Bottom of the Sea*, with Mash playing the part of everything that had ever swum in murky waters. She'd completed her look with sea-green-painted paws and claws, and was busy tossing a multitude of props into the cauldron, rhythmically chanting what sounded like the menu from the local Chinese takeaway. 'Tripe of beef, tongue of duck, ear of pig, feet of chicken, mix of kelp, grill of eel.'

'Brilliant, just brilliant,' shouted Micks. 'Now to me. Go on – say it for our visitors.'

Mash had been so taken with her role as all three hags that she'd hardly noticed her audience; when she did, she inadvertently slipped on a spillage of pea soup and rejuvenated her seaweed dreadlocks in the cauldron itself, saved only by Micks' quick action in pulling her out. Undaunted, she rose to her big speech, and Micks bowed his head to receive the oracle's news. 'Arise, Thane of Corduroy, King of Prawns, Noodle of Wonton, Master of Clams. Macbeth *shall* be King of Michaelmas!'

Hettie and Tilly stared in disbelief as Mash anointed Micks with a measuring jug full of pea soup, and both stepped forward to take a bow. Tilly could never resist a theatrical experience and clapped her paws in appreciation of the spectacle before her.

Hettie's was a more muted response, but the smile she offered was genuine.

'It's not *quite* there yet,' said Micks, 'but it wasn't too bad for a dry run, was it?'

The irony of the words didn't escape Hettie as she took in the full impact of the pea soup on the kitchen floor. 'I wonder if you could spare some time for a quick chat, Micks?' she said. 'I think you may be able to help us with our enquiries regarding the death up on the allotment yesterday.'

Micks threw his paws above his head and shrank back as if Hettie had run him through with a spear. 'Why should you think it was me? Why would I want to do that? Where's your evidence? That's what you'll need, evidence, and you won't find any round here.'

Mash adopted a pleading pose and fell down before Hettie with her paws clasped together. 'Oh, please don't take him! He's all I've got, and how will I manage without him? He's the love of my life.'

Hettie was finding the whole situation in the Wither-Spoons' kitchen more than a little wearing. She had never conducted an interview where the candidates were caked in pea soup before, and now they seemed to have left *Macbeth* behind in favour of the finer points of Victorian melodrama, with Micks assuming the role of dastardly villain and Mash as distressed damsel.

'Perhaps if we call back later that might be more

convenient to you both?' suggested Tilly, sensing that Hettie's patience was fast fraying at the edges.

Micks was about to respond when there was a loud and urgent hammering at the door. Startled, Mash slipped and fell backwards, banging her head on the cauldron as Micks slid his way to the door and hurled it open. Blackberry Tibbs stood in the doorway. 'I need the detectives!' she shouted. 'Jeremiah says he saw them coming in here. It's terrible!'

Deciding not to wait for any sort of response from Micks, Hettie and Tilly paddled through the pea soup and out into the sunshine, shutting the door behind them before Micks could follow. Blackberry was distraught, hopping from one paw to another, out of breath and gasping for air. Eventually, she managed some disconnected words: 'Lilies . . . blood . . . just lying there!' She jabbed her paw in the direction of the allotments.

Hettie and Tilly responded immediately. They crossed the road and took the central path to the allotments, where a hubbub of cats had gathered. The Chits were there, together with Bonny Grubb, the Mulch sisters, Tarragon Trench and Apple Chutney, but there was no time for conversation. Hettie stared down the path to where Jeremiah Corbit was standing at the gate to Gertrude Jingle's allotment. Blackberry caught up with them, still out of breath but a little more coherent. 'It's Miss Jingle,' she explained. 'She's been murdered. I found her when I went to collect the lilies. I've never seen so much blood!' The distressed cat collapsed onto the path and sobbed.

Hettie turned to the onlookers. 'Would one of you make Blackberry a nice cup of sweet tea? She's had a terrible shock and needs looking after. Tilly will stay with you and take statements while I go and see what's happened to Miss Jingle.' Tilly nodded in agreement, relieved to escape the initial viewing of the body; when it came to the grislier aspects of the detection business, she much preferred to take a back seat.

Hettie made her way down the path to Gertrude Jingle's gate, where Jeremiah Corbit was standing guard. 'It's not a pretty sight,' he said, as Hettie pushed past him, shutting the gate behind her. She was pleased and relieved to see Corbit turn on his heel and go back up the path without another word. The last thing she needed was a guided tour of the murder site by a cat who had questioned Miss Jingle's right to live there in the first place.

The beautiful white garden shone in the sunshine, with each bloom attracting as many bees as could fill its flower heads. The bees danced from one plant to another, collecting an abundance of late-summer pollen, and the joyful murmuring as they went about their work combined with an intoxicating scent to make what Hettie was about to see even more horrific. She followed the path up to the door of a small but attractive summer house, taking care to avoid treading on some delicate white lobelia that had strayed onto the old herringbone brickwork. The summer house boasted a veranda, with a single wooden chair and table to one side and a row of potted white geraniums to the other. The door in the centre was slightly ajar. Hettie stared at it for a moment, wishing that she could be anywhere else but in front of it. She knew that the peace and tranquillity of the garden had become a distorted and surreal entrance to the darkest of all crimes; just how dark she was about to find out.

She pushed the door open, and the true horror was immediate. The floor was strewn with white lilies, leading to a bed at the far end of the hut where Gertrude Jingle was sitting, propped up by her pillows. She was surrounded by more white lilies, but this time they were stained with blood, and her white nightdress was peppered with rips and tears where a knife had slashed and stabbed at her. The book she'd been reading had slipped from her bloodied paws and lay on the floor, stained beyond recognition; her spectacles were shattered and broken next to it, as if someone had ground them into the floor in a final act of spite.

In Hettie's experience, a body was supposed to take on the mantle of serenity in death – but not this time. In life, Miss Jingle had been a gentle cat of reduced circumstances, making the best of things and surrounding herself with flowers that could never hurt or disappoint her. Now, as Hettie took in the scene before her, it was as if the killer had wanted to mock her peaceful existence, as if they had actually enjoyed turning her home into a slaughterhouse, with the murdered cat as the ultimate centrepiece. She looked around, taking everything in. The walls were full of framed pictures: some were sepia photographs from the theatre, but most of the space was taken up with watercolours of flowers. An easel stood in one corner, with an abandoned paint-spattered smock draped across it and a collection of paints and coloured chalks on a small table next to it. Gertrude had clearly enjoyed painting flowers as well as growing them. In the opposite corner, there was a small log-burning stove and a high-backed rocking chair, well used and with an air of nobility about its intricately carved arms. A tartan rug lay abandoned on the seat of the chair, together with the remains of a slice of cake and half a mug of cocoa.

On first sight, Hettie had assumed that the cat had been murdered in her bed, but the half-eaten supper suggested something even more terrible. Had she let her killer in, then been subjected to some sort of horrendous ordeal before her life was taken from her? Had she been made to climb into her bed before the killer set to work? Had the book and the broken spectacles been added for effect? Whoever had done this would have left the scene covered in blood; even if the murder had taken place at night, the killer would surely have left some sort of trail? She returned to the garden, locking the summer-house door behind her to secure the scene from prying eyes – Miss Jingle deserved the dignity now that her killer had denied her. Blinded by the sunshine as she stepped out into the air, Hettie shaded her eyes with her paw and looked around her. On either side of the summer house was a collection of green water butts; behind it sat a small greenhouse, hidden from view. The water butts were as tall as Hettie, and she had to stand on tiptoes to look inside. Most of them contained clear, fresh rainwater, but the nearest had clearly been used to wash the blood off the killer's paws: the side of the butt was smeared with Gertrude's blood, where the killer had attempted to clean the evidence away.

The greenhouse offered further evidence: an abandoned bulb sack, still wet and covered in blood. Hettie looked round for further clues, finding a pile of empty sacks pushed under a potting bench. She pulled them out and, as she did so, a bloodstained handkerchief fell out of the sacks with a clank. The murder weapon, which had been hurriedly concealed in the sacking, was a long, pointed kitchen knife with a brown handle; except for the blood, the handkerchief was unmarked.

Hettie folded the handkerchief back over the knife

and placed it in one of the clean sacks, then returned to the summer house to see if Gertrude Jingle's cutlery bore any resemblance to the knife she'd found. In a drawer by the stove was a small collection of white-handled knives, forks and spoons, including two sharp kitchen knives; there was nothing that resembled the style of the murder weapon. Perhaps this was a stroke of luck: if Hettie could establish whose kitchen the murder weapon had come from, she might be closer to finding the killer. There was a long way to go, and she was yet to establish whether this murder had anything to do with the death of the stranger on Bonny Grubb's onion patch. She had a murder weapon, a pocketbook full of sketches and a whole community of cats who appeared to know nothing – but that was all. Without wasting any more time, she locked the door on the latest carnage, picked up her sack of evidence and went off to find Tilly.

CHAPTER ELEVEN

The sunshine could do nothing for the depression that had descended on the Wither-Fork allotments. Tilly had done her best to engage the community in general enquiries, but an air of silence and suspicion had taken over, and all the cats returned to the safety of their own patches of ground, declaring that they knew nothing about Miss Jingle's death.

'I think they're wondering who's next,' Tilly said, as Hettie caught up with her by Bonny Grubb's gate. 'I've spoken to Bonny, the Chits and Jeremiah Corbit so far, and had no luck with any of them. It seems that Miss Jingle kept herself to herself. Corbit said that if it hadn't been for Blackberry calling in to collect some lilies, Miss Jingle could have been undiscovered for days. I was just on my way to see Tarragon Trench.'

Hettie brought Tilly up to date with the rather macabre details of the murder, and the two cats let themselves in through the gate to Tarragon Trench's allotment. In the centre stood a tall wigwam tent surrounded by row after row of catnip plants at various stages of growth, and Hettie was impressed by the sheer quantity of what was viewed by some as an illegal substance. Used in small quantities, she had found it relaxing and therapeutic, and had had some of her best ideas after a pipe or two. For Tarragon Trench, it had become a way of life. He sat on a mat at the entrance to his tent, wearing a bright-yellow kaftan and plugged into a hubble-bubble pipe, which he puffed on as he stared up at the sky.

'Mr Trench,' she said, making her approach, 'I wonder if we might have a word with you?'

Tarragon continued to gaze up at the sky, but responded by treating Hettie and Tilly to an in-depth analysis of the current state of the universe. 'We all wonder about having words,' he said, 'but do we truly understand them, when they can change their shape and form by altering just one letter? They only exist when written down. They are nothing without the sky, the sea and the land to give them perspective. Words are but travellers along the way – said and forgotten, or misinterpreted to create wars where peace is just an obstruction. Words *unsaid* have power. They can be anything you want them to be.'

Hettie could see that there was no real point in even starting a conversation that was clearly going to waste time. With Trench continuing his catnip-fuelled musings, she and Tilly beat a hasty retreat back onto the path and opened the gate to Apple Chutney's allotment. After their rather strange encounter, the two cats were relieved to discover that Apple Chutney was almost normal. They found her lifting shallots and carefully placing them in wooden crates lined with newspaper, and she acknowledged their arrival with a cheerful smile that lit up her chocolate-brown face. She was dressed for gardening in a brightly patched pair of blue dungarees with a pair of heavy-duty gardeners' boots, adorned by red laces, and gave the impression of a cat who clearly inhabited her allotment in every sense of the word.

'I've decided to keep busy,' she said as they approached. 'I've always felt safe up here, and I even survived the great storm with only three jars of date and walnut lost and a bit of felting off me roof – but now I don't know *what* to think. Would you like to try a glass of beetroot pressé?'

Hettie's relationship with beetroot had never been a good one, and since Tilly had stained one of her best cardigans with a stray slice, she too had taken against it. They both declined Apple's offer of refreshment, keen to get on with the investigation. 'We were wondering whether you could help us with our enquiries into what has now become a double-murder investigation?' Hettie began. 'Perhaps you've noticed something or someone out of place up here in the last few days?'

Apple Chutney thought for a moment before replying, then slowly shook her head. 'Trouble is, I've been in me chutney shed mostly, so the world has passed me by in the last week or two. I've been getting me stock ready for the show. Miss Wither-Fork lets me have a stall in the marquee – she gets twenty per cent and I keep the rest.' Hettie looked around the allotment and noticed that there were two sheds, one painted bright red with curtains at the windows, and another that resembled a rounded grass hut with a large funnel-like chimney on its roof; a trail of brown smoke puffed up into the cloudless sky. Apple followed her gaze. 'That's me chutney shed. Come and have a look – I'm doing me final batches of sweet onion today.'

Hettie and Tilly followed the dungareed cat, taking care to avoid treading on any plants in their path, as almost every inch of soil on the carefully laid out allotment had been planted with vegetables or fruit bushes. The chutney shed was quite spacious inside and had the air of a small and very productive factory. The stove that supported the chimney had two large vats bubbling away on its hotplates. Beside the range were a number of neatly stacked crates of peeled onions, and the potting bench offered an assembly line of empty jars, lids and labels. 'Sorry about the smell,' said Apple, as their eyes began to stream from the pungent odour of onions, which filled their nostrils. 'You get used to it when you do it all day long.'

Hettie had seen enough and escaped into the sunshine, swiftly followed by Tilly. Apple stayed behind to heave a couple more crates of onions into the vats, eventually emerging with two jars of freshly made onion chutney. 'There you are,' she said. 'Should be lovely by Christmas. Just stick 'em in your cupboard. Go nicely with cold meats.'

Tilly tried to look grateful as Hettie forced the subject away from the chutneys and back onto the murder case. 'How do you get on with the other residents up here?' she asked, eyeing up the coiled barbed wire that crawled along the boundary fence.

'They're a nice bunch of cats, really,' Apple replied. 'I get on well with Blackberry. I grow pumpkins for her scarecrow heads, and that works well. I scoop the flesh for me creamed pumpkin puree and she has the outside skin to stuff for the heads. Come up like leather, they do. Last all winter.'

Hettie was beginning to wonder whether Apple had ever had a conversation that didn't include preserves, but pushed on with her interview, rephrasing the question. 'How do you get on with Jeremiah Corbit?'

The sunny disposition disappeared from Apple Chutney's face. Her whiskers drooped and she stared down at her boots. 'He's the worst thing about this place. Sometimes I wish one of his horrible compost heaps would swallow him up. He's a bully, and plain nasty with it. He thinks he's in charge up here, and he watches me when he thinks I'm not looking. It's creepy, really, and he hasn't got a good word to say for the others, either, especially the older cats like the Mulch sisters and Miss Jingle. Oh dear! I can't believe she's dead. Blackberry said she was stabbed hundreds of times. Why would anyone want to do that? She was an old cat who loved her flowers and kept herself to herself, although she was very partial to my seasonal piccalilli. She liked it with one of Mash Wither-Spoon's pork pies. Her cold water pastry's a triumph. Wins first prize at the show every year.'

Hettie was more than a little surprised to discover that Mash Wither-Spoon's talents ran to pork pies as well as very amateur dramatics, but she said nothing. It was time to move on. The very mention of pork pies reminded her that she and Tilly were invited to lunch at Wither-Fork Hall, and there were still cats to question on the allotments; the morning was slipping away from them. Saying their goodbyes and offering a polite thank you for the onion chutney, they left Apple to her shallots and returned to the path.

'Who's next?' asked Tilly, trying to cram the jars

of onion chutney into her cardigan pockets without much success.

'I think we'd better pay a call on Blackberry Tibbs to see how she is. The shock might be wearing off, in which case she may be able to shed some more light on Gertrude Jingle's death.'

Not wishing to cause further upset, Hettie left the sack containing the bloodied knife at Blackberry's gate. Tilly followed suit and divested herself of the chutneys, and the two cats entered the strange world of Blackberry Tibbs.

CHAPTER TWELVE

Hettie had been struck by the individuality of the allotments that she and Tilly had visited so far. The stark contrast of the Chits' homely existence with Jeremiah Corbit's bleak and colourless patch of land were perhaps the extremes, but the vision of what rose up before them on entering Blackberry Tibbs' plot could never have been predicted. 'Ooh look!' said Tilly, catching her breath. 'It's just like those Chinese cats made of pottery. Row after row of them, all different. How lovely!'

Hettie had to agree that the legion of scarecrows did indeed resemble a rather dishevelled version of the terracotta army, which they had recently seen on

TV. Unlike Tilly, she found the scale of Blackberry's endeavours rather alarming. 'I wouldn't want to be up here after dark with this lot,' she said, coming face-to-face with a figure that stared back at her through a bright-orange pumpkin mask.

The scarecrows were all of cat height and proportions, each secured to the ground on a single stake, which allowed the limbs to move freely. On closer inspection, it was clear that each scarecrow was as individual as any cat, and the clothes seemed to have been drawn from every century and every way of life. Tilly danced among them, marvelling at each new discovery. 'Look at this one,' she said, eyeing up a flamboyant cavalier who stood a head taller than she was. 'And here's an old-fashioned chimney sweep. Look over there at that shiny one – it's wearing a spacesuit, and this one looks like Top Cat.'

Not wanting to crush Tilly's enthusiasm, Hettie allowed her to wander among the scarecrows as she made her way towards an old railway carriage, set back from the assembled company. The maroon and black carriage was left over from the age of steam and boasted a platform at the front, complete with a number of scarecrows dressed as railway workers who could easily have stepped out of *Brief Encounter*, one of Tilly's favourite films. The face of Blackberry Tibbs stared from one of the many carriage windows as Hettie approached. She knocked on the central door and let herself in, not waiting for an invitation. Blackberry's swollen eyes and tear-stained face made it instantly clear that she had taken the discovery of Gertrude Jingle's body very hard indeed. She nodded to Hettie to sit on the bench seat opposite her own as she blew her nose and added the used tissue to a mountain of others on the floor by her feet. 'I'm sorry,' she said, looking across at Hettie. 'I expect you see nasty things like this every day in your work, but I just can't get the sight of poor Miss Jingle out of my head. I should try and pull myself together. I'm supposed to be up at the Hall cooking lunch, and Miss Wither-Fork needs to know what's happened.'

Hettie took in the interior of the carriage, noticing a neatly laid out galley kitchen at one end. 'Why don't we have a cup of tea, and then we'll all go up to the Hall and speak to Miss Wither-Fork,' she said, as Tilly made a perfectly timed entrance, bustling towards the small cooker in the galley to take up tea duties. Blackberry responded by blowing her nose again and pointing out that there were some chocolate finger biscuits in a tin by the tea caddy. Tilly filled the kettle from the small sink, located three mugs from one of the cupboards, and spooned tea into a brown, well-used teapot. The kettle, sensing the urgency, wasted no time in coming to the boil and sang its heart out briefly as Tilly prepared the mugs with milk and sugar.

When all three cats were settled with tea and biscuits, Hettie felt that this was a good moment to ask a few questions; it was some time since Blackberry had blown her nose, and Hettie took this as a signal to open her enquiries, nodding to Tilly to jot down any important responses in her notebook. 'I know this must be difficult for you,' she began, 'but could you run through the sequence of events that led you to the discovery of Miss Jingle's body?'

'I'll try,' said Blackberry, dipping a chocolate finger into her tea. 'When I collected the lilies from Miss Jingle yesterday, she told me to call in again this morning to pick up some more for the harvest festival arrangements in the church.'

'When is the harvest festival?'

'On Friday, Michaelmas Eve – the anniversary of Lettuce Wither-Fork's accident in the church. We all send some produce to decorate the altar on that day in celebration of her gift to us.'

'And what do you send?' asked Hettie, out of interest.

'I've got the best job,' said Blackberry, warming to her subject. 'I've recreated the whole of the Wither-Fork family from that time, including Lettuce. Miss Wither-Fork is letting me display them in the family pew.'

'As scarecrows!' exclaimed Tilly, still fascinated by the whole subject.

'Well, not exactly. The cats round here call my

figures scarecrows, but I like to think they're more than that. Very few of them end up scaring crows in fields. We have a scarecrow competition at the Michaelmas Show, and I make them to order for most of the residents up here. They come up with the ideas and I do the rest. It's fun to see whose idea wins.'

'What about all those lovely ones on your allotment?' asked Tilly. 'Are they for the show?'

'Not really. They're sort of in stock. I make a lot of them for theatres, or as extras in films when budgets won't run to paid actors – crowd scenes, mostly. I've done several zombie films and lots of dead bodies in battle scenes, too.'

At the mention of dead bodies, Blackberry was suddenly pulled back to the vision of Gertrude Jingle's corpse and felt the need to blow her nose again. Hettie seized the moment to ask another question. 'When I spoke to Miss Jingle yesterday, she said some very odd things about Micks Wither-Spoon – were they friends?'

'She had time for him,' said Blackberry, adding another sodden tissue to the pile. 'She loved the theatre, so she encouraged him and Mash with their plays. I think they made her laugh a lot. She used to say that watching one was a real tonic. She rarely left her lilies unless there was an event up at the Hall, and then she'd turn out in all her finery.'

'So what time did you go to Miss Jingle's allotment this morning?'

'It must have been about ten, because I saw the bus at the top of the hill. I looked for her in the garden at first, as her door was open and it was such a lovely sunny morning. I called out to her several times because she could be a bit deaf when she wanted to be, but there was no reply so I went towards the door. That's when I saw her.' Blackberry crumpled into a bout of sobs. Hettie waited patiently for the current wave of distress to subside while she caught up with two chocolate fingers, which were waiting to be dunked in her tea. Pulling herself together, and adding another tissue to the pile on the floor, Blackberry continued, 'It seems strange to think of it now, but it was the lilies that upset me. Miss Jingle loved her flowers, and to see them scattered all over the floor in such a violent way – and the blood, so much blood. I couldn't bear it. I just shut her door and ran down the allotment path, colliding with Jeremiah, who was coming out of his gate. I can't remember what I said to him, but he told me he'd seen you going into the gatehouse and said I should tell you what I'd found. He offered to stand guard at Miss Jingle's until I got back.'

Hettie drained her mug and Tilly collected them up and put them in the small sink, sliding open what she hoped would be the cutlery drawer. Glancing at the array of matching knives, forks and spoons, she could find nothing that resembled the weapon used to kill Miss Jingle; in fact, there was nothing with a wooden handle of any sort. Closing the drawer quietly, she passed down the carriage as Blackberry gathered herself to set out for Wither-Fork Hall. Hettie retrieved the sack and the chutneys which she'd left at Blackberry's gate, and the three cats adopted a brisk pace up the allotment path. They passed the gatehouse where Mash Wither-Spoon was grappling in the back garden with an unruly line of washing. She chased after them with her clothes prop in one paw and a bunch of letters in the other. 'If you're going up to the Hall you could save me a trip,' she said, catching up with them. 'These came for Fluff this morning – bills, mostly, by the look of them.' Blackberry took the letters and Mash returned to her laundry, behaving quite normally. Hettie made a mental note that the sooner she could pin the Wither-Spoons down to a proper interview, the better.

The grounds of Wither-Fork Hall were buzzing with excitement as tents were erected, car parks laid out, and a constant procession of tables, chairs and catering items unloaded from several vans. Hettie looked around at the scale of preparations for the Michaelmas Show, which was still three days away; already it seemed to be taking over most of the grounds in front of the Hall. As they drew closer to the industrious hubbub, the figure of Fluff Wither-Fork loomed large in the centre of the proceedings, directing and redirecting the army of cats who'd been enlisted to make her annual event a success.

Seeing Hettie, Tilly and Blackberry approaching, Fluff broke away from the workers to greet them. 'Good morning,' she said, every bit the baronial matriarch, but stopped dead at the look on Blackberry's face. 'Whatever's happened now? Please don't tell me there's more trouble.'

Hettie decided to save Blackberry from another painful explanation by bearing the bad news herself. 'I'm afraid it's Miss Jingle,' she said. 'She's been murdered during the night, and poor Blackberry here found her.' The air of authority dropped from Fluff Wither-Fork's face, and she visibly crumpled before them. Tilly stepped forward to prop her up. 'Shall we go back to the Hall?' Hettie suggested, wanting to shield Fluff's distress from a legion of onlookers.

'No, let's go to the church,' said Fluff, trying desperately to regain her composure. 'I've got to meet the vicar there in half an hour, and she's supposed to be coming to lunch.'

'Shall I go and get it ready?' offered Blackberry, not wishing to go through the discovery of Gertrude Jingle's body again and happy to leave that discussion to Hettie and Tilly.

'Yes please, Blackberry – that would be most helpful. The Reverend Stitch is a stickler for timekeeping, and she has a funeral at three back in the town.' At the mention of funerals, the landowner crumpled again, and this time both Hettie and Tilly came to the rescue, steering her towards the small church, which stood to the right of Wither-Fork Hall. Blackberry Tibbs, pleased to be off the hook, scampered back in the direction of the house to create a cheese and potato pie for which Fluff Wither-Fork would have no appetite.

CHAPTER THIRTEEN

St Wither-Fork's Church had stood for centuries, serving the family's religious and community needs. It was surrounded by a graveyard full of retainers and descendants, and the principal members of the family were laid to rest in an elaborate vault below the church floor. Hettie loved graveyards and was fascinated by the decorative architecture offered by most churches, but she had no time for what she regarded as the pomp and ceremony attached to the Gospels, which still seemed to dictate the lives of cats who chose to follow out-of-date doctrines. Loving your neighbour if you didn't like them seemed to Hettie a pointless exercise, and coveting their ox was even more ludicrous. It was the hypocrisy she hated most, the so-called divine right to set one cat above another in pursuit of a better place in the next life, and the ability of those who had given themselves that divine right to sit in judgement on others who refused to embrace their beliefs. The thought of sitting down to lunch with the Reverend Stitch had brought on a mild bout of indigestion – although one too many chocolate fingers from Blackberry's tin might also have been to blame.

The church was cold and gave off a strong smell of damp as the three cats entered; only the sunshine streaming through the stained-glass windows at the altar gave any colour to the place. The patterns of long-dead saints played out across the giant stone slab that marked the entrance to the Wither-Fork tomb in the centre of the floor. The rest of the church was laid out in neat rows of pews, with an elaborately carved stone font at the back, which had no doubt welcomed many a Wither-Fork kitten.

Hettie was about to offer the details of Gertrude Jingle's death to Fluff Wither-Fork when she noticed that they weren't alone. The front pew to the left of the altar was taken up with four cats, their heads slightly bowed in prayer or contemplation. Following her gaze, Fluff gave a nervous laugh. 'You can speak freely in front of them. They're all long dead and below the floor where we stand. What you see there is Blackberry's interpretation of Lettuce Wither-Fork and her kin. She's made them up especially for the harvest festival service and put them in the family pew.'

Tilly wasted no time in exploring Blackberry's models. They were frighteningly realistic – three male cats in medieval dress, and Lettuce herself in a sea-green gown with jewelled bodice and tiny silver slippers peeping out from the hem of her dress. The cat's face had a kind, noble air, and although Tilly wouldn't say it out loud, the model bore a definite resemblance to Fluff herself.

Hettie chose a pew at the back of the church and sat down to recount the morning's events. Fluff sat quietly, listening to the gory details and staring at the altar, lost in a grief that had more to do with herself than the death of one of her residents. Her response, when it finally came, weighed up the practicalities of the situation. 'Everything must be destroyed,' she said, taking Hettie by surprise. 'It was her wish to be cremated on her plot, along with all her flowers. She told me when she first came here that when she died that's how she wanted it to be. She said that fire purifies, and that she couldn't bear to leave her flowers behind as no one would love and care for them as much as she did.'

Gertrude Jingle's final wishes made perfect sense to Hettie. Her brief encounter with the dead cat had made it clear that she and her garden were one. Spiritually, it seemed rather a fine way to go, but she had been horribly snatched from her contented life and her killer was still out there somewhere, perhaps planning to strike again.

Hettie decided to address the issues of the case with Fluff before the imminent arrival of the Reverend Stitch. 'We've been slightly derailed by Miss Jingle's murder,' she said, as Tilly joined them in the pew. 'The dead stranger may or may not be connected to the latest murder, but my concern is that other cats could be at risk. It might be best for all concerned if you cancelled the Michaelmas Show, or at least postponed it until the killer's caught.'

'That's impossible,' said Fluff. 'I'll be bankrupt if I cancel, and what about all the cats who depend on me? Wither-Fork Hall is finished, and all of us who live here if we don't get the revenue from the show.'

'Maybe that's the point,' said Tilly, in a rare outspoken moment. Hettie and Fluff shot a look at her.

'What do you mean?' Hettie asked.

'Well, if the killer killed the stranger, thinking that the show would be cancelled and it wasn't, then if they thought by killing again it would be cancelled, that would be a good reason for doing it twice. If they still haven't managed to stop the show, they may kill again, or they may think that by killing again the show still won't be cancelled so they won't bother. So there doesn't seem much point in cancelling the show, otherwise cats have been killed for nothing and everyone loses, not just the cats who've been killed already.'

Fluff Wither-Fork and Hettie continued to stare at Tilly, both trying hard to follow her logic. They were mercifully interrupted by the thick oak door of the church being barged open. A portly, wheezing, long-haired ginger cat stood in the doorway, instantly recognisable from the white collar that wrapped itself tightly around her neck, making every attempt to confine the cleric's triple chins. Seeing that she had a congregation of seven, including the effigies of the long-dead Wither-Forks, she instantly kicked into vicar mode, using the acoustics of the church to enhance her sing-song voice. 'Good morning to all, and such a glorious one, too. God has seen fit to bless us with this joyful day that we may go about His work with an open heart in thankful praise of the life He has given us. Or, as I said to the young cat during my weekly broadcast on our local radio station, God moves in mysterious waves!'

Refusing to acknowledge the joke, Hettie could barely resist pointing out that the carnage she had left on the allotment was hardly a blessing *or* her idea of a joyful day, but she chose to remain silent. The Reverend Augusta Stitch performed her genuflections at the altar before addressing the company once again. 'Now then, are we all ready for the harvest festival?' she enquired, adopting her school assembly voice. 'Two days to go and none of Miss Jingle's lilies, I see. Has there been a mix-up with the flower arrangers? I thought Miss Tibbs was collecting the lilies this morning? A bit behind, are we? We mustn't get carried away with the show, not before the harvest festival service.' At this point, she broke into her favourite harvest hymn, and Fluff, Hettie and Tilly could do nothing but stare as she wheezed her way through several verses of 'We Plough the Fields and Scatter', twirling her way down the aisle of the church towards the altar, where she finally came to rest on a red velvet kneeler.

Feeling the need to regain her sanity, Hettie rose from the pew and signalled to Tilly that they were leaving. Assuring Fluff that they would return to the Hall in time for lunch, the two cats left the landowner in the sacred company of the wheezing mass at the altar and fled out into the sunshine.

CHAPTER FOURTEEN

'Micks and Mash Wither-Spoon next,' said Hettie, turning her face to the sun as they left the cold, clammy atmosphere of St Wither-Fork's. 'A conversation with those two is long overdue. They seem to have a claw in all the pies around here, and I doubt there's much they miss up at the gatehouse.'

'I wonder who they're being now?' responded Tilly, making a beeline for a doughnut stall, which seemed to be having a practice run. The cats watched as the doughnuts swirled in the hot fat, giving off that unmistakable smell of sizzling sweet batter, and were both rewarded with a doughnut, which the stallholder tossed in a mountain of white sugar and cinnamon.

Tilly paid up as several of the helpers formed an orderly queue behind her. The practice run was proving a popular mid-morning distraction for the cats engaged in the Michaelmas Show preparations.

'Oooh lovely!' said Tilly, covering her whiskers, ears and the top of her head in sugar. 'Almost as good as Beryl's, and extra nice to eat them outside.' Hettie had to agree. There was something special about outdoor food: the fresh air and lack of conformity made it almost forbidden fruit, although Hettie had never been a fan of fruit of any kind unless it was wrapped in pastry or sponge.

The friends crossed in front of the Hall and made their way up to the gatehouse, where Mash Wither-Spoon was watering a collection of brightly coloured pansies in her backyard. She turned to acknowledge them with a wide and welcoming smile. 'Fancy a cup of tea to wash those doughnuts down?' she said, making it clear that she'd been watching their progress across the parkland. 'You wait till the show on Saturday. Every tasty treat your heart can desire: hot dogs, burgers, toffee apples, candyfloss, and then there's the food tent. My sister prides herself on that. After the judging, all the pies, pastries and hams are up for grabs – bargains galore and a positive stampede, although the veg is always left, even if it has won a prize. Mind you, that's if the show goes ahead at all.'

'Why do you say that?' asked Hettie, as she and Tilly followed Mash into her kitchen.

'I'd have thought that was obvious,' said Mash, filling the kettle. 'Two murders and heaven knows what's to come. Fluff is batting on a bit of a sticky wicket if you ask me. I don't know why she does it to herself. Micks has offered to run the estate for her, but for some reason she just won't have it.' From what Hettie had seen of Micks Wither-Spoon, she could perfectly understand why Fluff might be reticent to leave the estate in his paws, but she said nothing and Mash continued, 'He drew up a lovely plan and presented it to her in the spring, just after all the winter bills had come in, but she wouldn't have it. All this business over duty and Lettuce Wither-Fork and her charity.'

'What was the plan?' asked Hettie, settling herself at the kitchen table and taking care to avoid the pools of green slime left over from the *Macbeth* run-through.

'A theme park!' replied Mash. 'They're all the rage these days. With Blackberry's models and our theatrical expertise, we could really have put Wither-Fork Hall on the map, but she just wouldn't have it. Micks and I washed our paws of her after that, and we live a lovely life here at the gatehouse – when she's not telling us off, that is.'

Hettie secretly admired the idea of a theme park, but completely understood why Fluff Wither-Fork had vetoed it. It was mainly due to Micks, no doubt, but there was also a noble air of going down with her ship about the chatelaine of Wither-Fork Hall, and it had to be admired, no matter how self-destructive it might prove.

Mash made four mugs of tea, putting two of them in front of Hettie and Tilly. She made up a tray with one of the others, added a large slice of pork pie, then headed for the stairs in the corner of the kitchen. 'I'll just pop this up to Micks,' she said. 'He's learning his lines in the turret. Back in a minute – help yourselves to sugar.'

'Well, that was a bit interesting,' said Tilly, satisfied that Mash was out of earshot. 'I think a theme park is a really good idea. They could have had those re-enactments where cats take sides and pretend to be dead. You know – with cavaliers and roundheads, like the sealed nits do.'

Hettie spat a mouthful of tea across the table. 'Knot! Sealed knot!' she corrected. 'And there's no need for cats to pretend round here. We already have some who are *properly* dead.'

'Who's properly dead?' asked Mash, reappearing from the stairs. 'Not another one, surely?'

'No, just the two for now,' said Hettie, sounding weary. 'I would like to ask you and Micks some questions about the murders, though, if you have time?'

'I'm not sure how much time Micks has got, as he's panicking over his Thane of Corduroy soliloquy, but I've got the hags and Lady M off to a T so I can answer for him. He's not a great conversationalist unless he's pretending to be someone else.'

Tilly opened her notebook, and Hettie began. 'Miss Jingle told me that you have a good vantage point across the allotments from your turret.'

'We do, and across to the Hall as well. It was designed to give advance warning of conquering armies in days gone by. Micks loves it up there. It makes him feel like the king of the castle. We keep all our costumes there, too, like a proper theatre wardrobe department.'

'You're obviously aware of the stranger found dead on Bonny Grubb's onion patch,' Hettie continued, refusing to discuss theatre or wardrobes. 'Did either of you see anything from the turret that might be of help in identifying him?'

'Not that I can think of, but we can't see much of Bonny's patch from here, not even with Micks' binoculars. She's right up the top end.'

'And what about Miss Jingle?'

'Well, I couldn't say what *she* might have seen. Didn't you ask her?'

Hettie was confused for a moment, but put the question a different way. 'I meant did you or Micks see anything that might help us with the murder of

Miss Jingle? I understand that she took an interest in Micks and his plays.'

Mash, visibly irritated, sidestepped the question. 'Oh, and which one of that lot is telling tales out of school? Most of them never miss an opportunity to have a go at poor Micks, and even Miss Jingle could be cruel sometimes. Blackberry's the only decent one among them. At least she's kind to him.'

Hettie responded with the shock news that it was, in fact, Blackberry who had given her the information. 'Then if it's come from Blackberry, that's all right. Miss Jingle *had* been helping Micks with his lines – she was good at that sort of thing. She suggested *Macbeth*, actually. She said it would suit us both, as the parts were engrossing and Wither-Fork Hall was the perfect setting.'

'You said Miss Jingle could be cruel to Micks. In what way?'

'She sometimes sent him notes after our performances. She never missed one, but she could be quite discouraging at times. She was really horrible about Micks' Joan of Arc. She said he was more like Guy Fawkes than the Maid of Orleans when it came to the burning scene, and I wouldn't mind but he put a lot into that. She did say my Dauphine was exceptional, though, so it wasn't all bad.'

Reluctant to delve much further into the Wither-Spoons' theatrical adventures, there was nevertheless one question that Hettie wanted to ask out of pure curiosity. 'Why does Micks play so many female cat roles?'

Mash gave a haughty laugh. 'You're clearly not au fait with the Bard. Any cat who aspires to treading the boards knows that Mr Shakespeare would have no truck with female cats, and gave all the parts to males. Micks likes to be as authentic as possible, unless he prefers the male role for himself.'

'And what about you? Will you be playing Lady Macbeth?'

'Of course, but Micks is wearing her gowns, as he says she's got the best costumes. I get to wear doublet, hose and chain mail – or rather tin foil, as we've had to improvise since our Gawain and the Green Knight ended up in the ornamental pond after the jousting tournament.'

Tilly stifled a giggle, and Hettie returned to the subject of Gertrude Jingle's death. 'Could you tell me if Micks visited Miss Jingle yesterday?'

Mash looked affronted at such an obviously loaded question. 'I hope you're not suggesting that Micks had anything to do with Gertrude's death? I thought she died in the night.'

'Where did you hear that?' asked Hettie.

Mash looked flustered. 'I don't know. I think I just assumed it. He did call in to see her, but she was fine when he left. He got back about six, and look – she sent me those lilies for Lady Macbeth's bower.'

Hettie was puzzled as she stared at the lilies by the sink. They looked abandoned and desperate for water. 'I really would like a quick word with Micks, if that's possible,' she said. 'Besides the killer, he was probably the last cat to see Miss Jingle alive.'

Mash gave a huge sigh. 'I don't think you fully understand. Micks is a special sort of cat, and not like you and me. He creates his own worlds and lives in them. He's quite fragile, really. I don't think he *really* believes that Miss Jingle is dead. He probably thinks it's all part of a play.'

'Then perhaps he'd like to come with me to see the body,' suggested Hettie, refusing to be fobbed off. 'It's the best bit of theatre he'll ever see, and it might just jog his memory. He might notice something of vital importance to the case – something out of place, perhaps, that could lead us to the killer.'

Mash froze at the thought of subjecting Micks to such an ordeal. 'What you suggest is out of the question. He's not fit enough to deal with anything like that. He has tremors that last for days when he's upset – can't hold a cup of tea or anything. I've told you all we know, and I suggest you look closer to home for your killer. The Mulch sisters had quite a difficult relationship with Gertrude, and Jeremiah Corbit couldn't stand her. Now, if you'll excuse me, I have to get on with my ironing.'

'Just one more thing,' said Hettie, opening the sack that had become her constant companion. 'Do you recognise this knife?'

Mash stared in horror, visibly shaken. 'Is that what killed Miss Jingle?' Hettie nodded, and Mash's eyes filled with tears. She shook her head slowly. 'No, I've never seen it before.'

Mash Wither-Spoon rose from her kitchen table, making it clear that the conversation was over. Hettie and Tilly left her snatching laundry off the washing line in her backyard, and made their way back to Wither-Fork Hall for Blackberry Tibbs' cheese and potato pie.

CHAPTER FIFTEEN

Blackberry greeted them at the door, and this time she showed Hettie and Tilly into Fluff Wither-Fork's private rooms below stairs. The parlour was a far cry from the faded splendour of the baronial dining room, but it was comfortable and welcoming. A round table in the centre of the room was set for four, and Hettie remembered with a groan that the Reverend Stitch would be breaking bread with them. 'Make yourselves comfortable,' said Blackberry. 'Miss Wither-Fork's showing the vicar a painting she wants to sell. They won't be long.'

'There is one small thing you could help with,' said Hettie, wrestling the knife out of the sack she carried. 'Does this resemble any of the knives in Miss Wither-Fork's kitchens?'

Blackberry shrank back from the weapon, instantly distressed, then moved in for a closer look. 'It does seem familiar, but there's so much stuff in the kitchens here. You should ask Bonny Grubb – she sharpens all the knives for the Hall. She kept her dad's sharpening stones, and no one sharpens a knife like an old Gypsy tinker. It's in her blood.'

At the mention of the word 'blood', Blackberry made a hasty exit for the kitchens to wrestle the pie from the Aga, leaving Hettie and Tilly to perch on a battered but comfortable sofa in the parlour. 'It's much nicer in here,' said Tilly. 'Much better than that barn of a dining room upstairs. Fluff must be quite cosy with all her lovely things around her. These big old houses are quite nasty, really – cold, damp and impossible to decorate with all those high ceilings. Just think how much polish you'd use if you took on that big staircase. I don't know why Fluff Wither-Fork doesn't buy a nice little house in Whisker Terrace.'

'Neither do I some days,' said Fluff as she came into the parlour, much to Tilly's embarrassment. 'But as things stand at the moment, I couldn't afford a caravan on Southwool beach, let alone a house in Whisker Terrace.'

'Well, you can put that fifty pounds towards your deposit,' boomed the Reverend Stitch, following Fluff through the door. 'I'm a fool for a Madonna and Kitten, and that painting will be perfect in my study at the rectory.'

'I'm glad you like it,' said Fluff. 'But I'm afraid the money will go to pay the bills, and I haven't yet agreed a fee for all the work that Miss Bagshot and her assistant are doing on the murders.'

Hettie was pleased to hear that their fee hadn't been forgotten. At Fluff's invitation, she and Tilly took their place at the table just as Blackberry arrived with a large cheese and potato pie.

The Reverend Stitch wobbled with excitement, making Tilly think that she was sitting by a giant living jelly. Hettie was relieved to be next to Fluff, who wasted no time in putting four large helpings of the pie onto the plates and passing them round the table. Blackberry returned to the kitchen, leaving the diners to enjoy the fruits of her labours.

Hettie lifted her fork and instantly put it down again as Augusta Stitch rose from the table to inflict grace on the rest of them. It was just as well that the pie was hot, as the thank yous addressed to her maker went on for some time. The Reverend finally sat down and demolished her pie before Tilly had barely managed her first forkful. Hettie took her time with her own portion, savouring every mouthful, but Fluff just picked at hers, moving it absent-mindedly round the plate.

Augusta filled her plate twice more before leaning back in her chair like a satisfied walrus, putting yet more strain on her clerical collar and the chair. After much cleaning, wheezing and appreciative grunting, the vicar finally focused on her fellow diners. 'So, Miss Bagshot, what's to be done? Satan's abroad, and you are charged with eradicating his works and bringing him to justice. Let's hope that no more of our Lord's flock will suffer in the meantime. Miss Wither-Fork tells me you have a track record of solving such atrocities, and one feels you walk in the shadow of death. Let us pray you fear no evil, as the good book says.'

Hettie couldn't resist this time and replied as only she knew how. 'My main concern, if I *was* a believer, would be why God allows such atrocities in the first place. My experience has shown me that victims of murder are usually blameless and without sin, and the perpetrators live lives embedded in evil, which enables them to do what they do. To make matters worse, it's the murderers that history remembers. If Satan exists, under those circumstances he's on the winning side.'

Fluff Wither-Fork and Tilly stared at Hettie in admiration as the Reverend Augusta Stitch checked her watch and rose from the table like a cat who had been well and truly slapped. 'I must get going,' she said. 'Funerals wait for no cat. Will you be requiring a service for Miss Jingle?'

Fluff responded with another blow. 'I'm afraid not.

Miss Jingle had alternative ideas regarding her funeral. There is to be an open-air cremation on her allotment. She was sceptical regarding religion of any sort. I shall leave the arrangements to Morbid Balm from Shroud and Trestle. Don't forget your painting – it's by the front door.' She waited for the footsteps to die away before releasing a tirade of abuse at her departing lunch guest. 'Insufferable despot! Holier than thou, without an ounce of humility about her. She thinks she has us all under the cosh with her patronising view of humanity. If it wasn't for Christmas, Easter and the harvest festival I'd set the hounds on her – if we had any. Thank God it's only three times a year! *And* she charges for petrol on top of her fee for that ludicrous bread van she drives about in. Her church in the town is half-empty most Sundays, such is her magnetic draw for the parishioners, and I gather the Baptists are doing extra business because of her. Bring back the Reverend Mulch, that's what I say.' Fluff suddenly became aware of the look of appreciation on Hettie's and Tilly's faces and decided not to apologise for her outburst, which had clearly met with the approval of her remaining guests.

'I fear there is much to be discussed,' said Fluff, encouraging Hettie and Tilly to sit on the sofa as Blackberry entered on cue to clear the table. 'I should tell you how much I appreciate your involvement in these terrible murders, and due to the sale of a painting I loathed, I'm in the happy position to offer you twenty pounds on account, if that is acceptable?'

Hettie and Tilly sat up straight at the mention of money, ready to sharpen their pencils for some concentrated work. 'Twenty pounds would be very acceptable,' said Hettie, pleased to know that the Butters' rent was now safe for the foreseeable future. At two pounds per week, plus coal and luncheon vouchers, they could almost coast to Christmas on the fee from what would come to be known as The Michaelmas Murders. At this point, though, there was no hope of a 'case solved', and considerably more digging would be needed before the fee was properly earned. As far as Hettie and Tilly were concerned, the plot was soon to thicken and even more trouble awaited them in the wings.

After the various conversations of the morning, Hettie's head was full of questions that she felt Fluff could help with. 'Miss Wither-Fork,' she began, while Tilly chose a clean page in her notebook, 'we've just come from a rather odd conversation with your sister, who is refusing to allow us to talk to Micks about the murders. She seems to think that he's incapable of dealing with anything, and is obviously protecting him.'

'Well, there's nothing odd about that. Micks *is* incapable, and Mash has made it her life's work to shield him from the outside world. It's a cross she's chosen to bear and it frustrates the hell out of the rest of us, but – in her defence – there are reasons, if you've time?' Hettie nodded, and Fluff continued, 'Micks was raised in a theatrical family. At one time, his parents were the toast of seaside entertainment, and Micks travelled with them from theatre to theatre. He was born in a trunk – literally – during the interval of a matinee performance of *The Mikado*, hence his name. The story goes that Micks' parents were attacked in their dressing room after a Saturday evening show. I think they'd been doing a modern interpretation of *A Midsummer Night's Dream*, or something like that. Anyway, Micks was in his trunk, where he slept, and witnessed the whole gory business. They were beaten and stabbed to death, and to make matters worse the killer escaped, locking the door behind him and taking the key. Micks was in the dressing room with the bodies for two days – the theatre staff only found him when they returned to the building on Monday for the next performance. As far as I know, the killer was never caught. Being very young, Micks was shattered by the experience and never got over it. Mash met him on a method-acting course years later, and it would appear that they each found their soulmate. He's a sad case, really, but Mash controls him reasonably well, and they do lead a carefree life – mostly at my expense.'

'Mash mentioned that they'd offered you a rescue package to save the estate recently,' said Hettie. 'She seemed upset that you'd refused. Is there trouble between you?'

'I'm surprised she mentioned the theme-park scheme to you at all. It was a novel idea, but it would have needed pots of money to get it off the ground, and with Micks and Mash at the helm, goodness knows what would have happened. They came up with it because I panicked them into thinking they might be homeless.'

'Why was that?'

'As you know, we had a very harsh winter. By the time we got to the spring, I was up to my neck in fuel bills and ready to throw the towel in. As I mentioned to you yesterday, I wrote begging letters to various organisations in the hope that someone with money would take the house on, but I had no luck there so I soldiered on, selling the paintings off the walls and the rugs from the floors. I think Micks and Mash came up with the theme-park scheme to stop me giving them and the estate away. We can but dream.'

'Would they have been made homeless if you'd found someone to take the estate on?'

'Not really. They're sitting tenants, but a new owner – as long as they provided alternative accommodation on the estate – could easily see them out of the gatehouse. The same goes for the allotments. Lettuce's legacy makes it clear that the residents should be housed on the estate, but the allotments weren't there in her time so I imagine they could also be moved. But that's hypothetical, as no one wants to take the place on any way. I would never dream of turning Micks and Mash out, although I won't say I haven't been tempted at times.'

'Nobody on the allotments seems to like Jeremiah Corbit,' said Hettie, opening up a new subject. 'What's your opinion of him?'

'Corbit? One of life's losers, I think. He strives for something that isn't there and doesn't know the meaning of the word contentment, and he needs to feel in charge even though he isn't. He's definitely the wasp in the woodpile up there. He's made poor Apple Chutney's life a misery at times, and as for the barbed wire – if I've told him once I've told him a thousand times to take it down. It makes us look like a concentration camp. He asks for a meeting with me once a month to discuss "the state of the allotments", to use his words. He seems to think I've appointed him as some sort of bailiff, and he uses those meetings to tear the rest of the residents to shreds. I just pretend to listen and send him back to his ghastly compost heaps.'

'Do you think he's capable of murder?'

'Well, that's a difficult one. He strikes me as the sort who prefers his victims to be alive – that way, he can continue to taunt them.'

'And what about the rest of them? Any potential

there?' asked Hettie, keen to get Fluff's personal overview of her tenants.

Fluff thought for a moment before answering. 'The Gamp sisters are harmless enough. Bonny is dishonest as the day is long, but I doubt she could even kill a rabbit for the pot. Tarragon Trench is rather strange – I suppose he *could* be capable of murder during one of his catnip-fuelled episodes, but he's the sort who would confess as soon as he'd done it, and he *does* play the organ for us in church, which requires a certain amount of sensitivity. Apple Chutney has sad days, when she locks herself in her chutney shed – no one knows why, but I suspect that Jeremiah has something to do with it. If Gertrude hadn't died, I could easily have believed her capable of murder, especially if she was defending her flowers. There was a bit of a set-to regarding the Mulch sisters' earwigs, and more than a few insults flew over the fence there. Come to think of it, the Mulches have an air of arsenic and old lace about them, and they did wage war on the rectory garden when Augusta Stitch took over from their father. Dug up the dahlias at the dead of night, I gather. I could easily see them working as a murderous team, but killing a perfect stranger and then setting about Gertrude in such a violent way is perhaps more Agatha Crispy than Dahlia and Gladys Mulch.'

Tilly giggled at the mention of one of her favourite

crime writers. 'The Chits are a joy to have up there,' Fluff continued. 'No trouble at all, the perfect little family. I doubt that they would add to their past sorrow by murdering anyone. And as for Clippy Lean and Blackberry Tibbs, they're both made of the salt of this earth. Clippy would put herself out to help any cat in trouble, and Blackberry – well, she's my rock, always cheerful, discreet and very talented. Her plot on the allotments is a showpiece. She could work anywhere, but she chooses to stay at Wither-Fork and that never ceases to amaze me.'

It had occurred to Hettie that Blackberry's talents were wasted at Wither-Fork Hall, but she said nothing, aware that the cat was busy in the kitchen next to the parlour and – like all good servants – had probably been listening in on their conversation. 'The stranger is a real mystery,' she said. 'The notebook we salvaged from Bonny had sketches in it, as if he was on some sort of drawing holiday. I noticed that Miss Jingle was fond of painting, and I wondered if there was a connection? Did she ever have friends or family come to visit?'

Fluff shook her head. 'Not that I know of. She seemed to have drawn a very thick line under her past life. I think the losing of her fortune was just too painful. She delighted in her allotment and took great joy in the special events here at the Hall, especially if Micks and Mash were giving a performance –

she loved a drama of any kind. And speaking of drama, if you have no further questions you'll have to excuse me. I must call Shroud and Trestle, and see if Morbid Balm can organise a cremation for tomorrow, otherwise Gertrude's funeral will have to wait until after the weekend. Friday will be taken up with the harvest festival, and the show is on Saturday. If Morbid can't accommodate us tomorrow, we're looking at Monday, and that will be the big clear-up day, if all goes to plan.'

Hettie and Tilly stood to leave, and Fluff – true to her word – put twenty pounds into Hettie's paw. 'Please keep me up to date on your progress,' she said, showing them out of the parlour. 'I expect you'll want to attend the funeral, so I'll call your office later to confirm times. Feel free to come and go as you please, and if I can be of any further assistance, just shout.'

As Hettie stowed away the twenty-pound note in the pocket of her business slacks, she encountered the key to Gertrude Jingle's summer house. Pulling it out, she proffered it to Fluff. 'Morbid Balm will need this to prepare Miss Jingle for her funeral. I locked the place up to stop anyone going in there – no one should see what's been done to her unless they have to.'

Fluff took the key and stared at it with great sadness. 'Someone's going to have to take on the task of digging up all Gertrude's lilies,' she said with a deep sigh. 'She specifically asked that they should be burnt with her. I think that's a job for Rooster Chit. He's wonderful in a crisis.'

'She obviously believed in planning ahead,' said Hettie as they reached the front door. 'Was she concerned for her safety, do you think?'

Fluff considered the question. 'No, I don't think so. She'd been through the trauma of losing her home, and I think her main concern when she came to Wither-Fork was to put permanent roots down, or in her case lily bulbs. I think she was just being far-sighted in her funeral plans, especially as they are a little out of the ordinary.'

Hettie and Tilly left Fluff to her funeral arrangements and stepped out into the afternoon sunshine. The day was still glorious, and as Hettie looked around her she noted that much progress had been made in the preparations for the Michaelmas Show. Sadly, the present case for the No. 2 Feline Detective Agency seemed to be making very little progress at all.

CHAPTER SIXTEEN

'Where do we go from here?' asked Tilly, cleaning her whiskers after a particularly sticky strawberry milkshake. 'My notebook is nearly full up and I'm not sure there's anything helpful in it at all.'

Hettie lay back with her paws behind her head, enjoying the sunshine after putting away a mint chocolate chip ice cream tub in record time. The vendors were growing in number on the parkland, and, with money in their pockets, Hettie had decided that an afternoon snack was appropriate. 'I think we have to go right back to the beginning,' she said, eventually answering Tilly's question. 'This all kicked off with a dead cat on Bonny Grubb's onion patch. Maybe Bonny knows more than she's saying. We need to talk to her about the knife, so I think a bit more probing wouldn't go amiss. The Mulch sisters interest me, too. I think we should have another chat with them this afternoon, and then we should go home and thrash out the stuff in your notebook. We've collected a lot of facts, but I think we need some time to string them together. I can't help but feel that someone must have missed the stranger by now, and he may be the key to everything. The trouble is, every cat involved in this mess is either hiding or running away from something.'

'What do you mean?'

'Well, most of the folk up on the allotments treat their plots as some sort of sanctuary. They all seem to have a history, which they're keen to bury along with their vegetables: the Chits are grief-stricken; Corbit carries his guilt like a self-harming exercise; Apple Chutney is obsessed with preserving things and suffers from low moods in her chutney shed, so that smacks of a difficult past; Tarragon Trench cushions himself from the outside world with a constant overdose of catnip; and as for the Mulch sisters – goodness knows what skeletons live in their cupboards, but they're very keen to justify their existence up there.'

'What about Clippy Lean and the Gamps?' asked Tilly, admiring Hettie's psychological profiling.

'They're the exception to the rule. As Corbit said,

they just wanted a bit of extra garden to grow flowers and vegetables.'

'And what about Bonny? What's she running away from?'

'At a guess, I'd say the open road. There was a time when the annual arrival of a Gypsy camp put a town or village on red alert. They were all tarred with the same brush – thieves, murderers and abductors of young female cats. As the Gypsy families broke up and scattered for one reason or another, life on the road must have become a very lonely place. Bonny does as she likes up there, and although she wouldn't admit it, she's part of a community that resembles an old Gypsy camp without the hassle of being run out of town whenever the silver goes missing. She's a great one for telling the old stories. Bruiser and I used to sit round her campfire night after night before the great storm hit.'

'Maybe *we* should have an allotment,' said Tilly, suddenly remembering how nice the Chits' boathouse was. 'We could build our own shed to live in and keep the Butters' back room as an office.'

'I don't think we'd fit the criteria,' said Hettie, shuddering at the thought of sharing a boundary fence with Jeremiah Corbit. 'And anyway, we hate most vegetables, so why would we want to grow them? Living with the Butters, we've got the best pies in town on tap.'

Tilly had to agree, and the two friends struck out for the allotments before succumbing to the temptations of another vendor who had just started frying sausages on his griddle. There was no sign of Micks or Mash as they passed the gatehouse, and on reaching the allotment path all was peaceful. Bonny Grubb was fast asleep in an old deckchair by her caravan, and Hettie couldn't resist peering over the gate to the Gamp sisters' plot; there was no sign of them, so she lifted the latch on their gate, more out of curiosity than purpose.

Tilly followed her in, and both cats stared in great amusement at the sight before them. The Gamp sisters were famous in the town for their synchronicity. They were identical short-haired black cats who wore matching clothes, said the same things at the same time, and generally lived their lives in tandem. Everyone knew them, and yet no one knew anything about them. No one that Hettie had come across even knew their first names, although they were bound to be the same.

Their allotment could not have belonged to anyone else. The plot was divided into two narrow strips of land, each boasting an identical shed at the top end. In front of the sheds were two small patio areas, peppered with pots of geraniums, and Tilly noted that there were two pink, two red and two white flowers in each, all in corresponding positions. Then came the vegetables:

three rows of potatoes; three rows of feathery carrots; an onion patch, four rows deep by seven sets across; two marrow plots sporting four marrows each; and, to finish, two rows of flourishing red-veined beetroot plants. The strips of land were planted in matching quantities, and – remarkably – the plants had grown to the same height, as if sensing the importance of conforming in every way. At the bottom of the plots stood matching water butts and wheelbarrows, and beyond them two matching compost heaps.

Having taken in the bizarre, pedantic perfection of the Gamps' patch of land, Hettie and Tilly returned to the path and headed down towards the Mulch sisters, hoping for some sanity amid the strange world of the Wither-Fork allotments. It was clearly washing day on the estate. The Mulch sisters had followed Mash Wither-Spoon's example and were busily pegging out an assortment of clothes on a line that stretched from their hut to a small cherry tree on the boundary with Gertrude Jingle's plot. Dahlia Mulch mumbled a greeting through a mouthful of pegs, and Gladys stood by, selecting and passing wet clothes to her sister from a laundry basket.

Hettie stood and waited while they completed their task before wading in with her first question. 'I'm sorry to bother you both again,' she said, 'but I wonder if you could tell me where you both were last night?' She had decided to go for the jugular and her question produced the desired effect. Gladys dropped her empty laundry basket and Dahlia looked visibly shaken, almost swallowing the remaining peg that stuck out through her front teeth.

Gaining her composure, Gladys was the first of the sisters to speak. 'What business is it of yours where we were?' she countered. 'We've already made it clear to your assistant that we know nothing, and that should be an end to it.'

Hettie couldn't help but notice the change in tone from their last meeting. Gone were the sweet old cats dressed in flower-print frocks, pottering about in their tidy little shed with a stew bubbling on the stove. Now, the Mulch sisters looked confrontational and Dahlia picked up where her sister had left off. 'All we ask is to be left in peace to go about our business like we always have. That's all we've got to say.'

She turned on her heel, moving towards the shed, but stopped in her tracks as Hettie went in for the kill. 'You are our number-one suspects for the murder of Gertrude Jingle, and for that reason we have more questions to ask you. It may be that we can eliminate you from our enquiries, but at the moment you're at the top of the list.'

Gladys and Dahlia Mulch stood rooted to the spot like two of Blackberry Tibbs' scarecrows. Even Tilly was shocked by Hettie's aggressive approach, but it did bear fruit. Once again, it was Gladys who responded first, this time turning on the charm. 'Oh, do forgive us for our anger, but we are in deep shock. Our world has been turned upside down by these murders, and I assure you that we had nothing to do with poor Gertrude's death.'

Recovering herself, Dahlia followed her sister's example. 'We were both in our shed all evening and retired early to bed to listen to a classical concert on the radio. We'd been looking forward to it all week.'

'And what was the concert?' pressed Hettie, determined to keep the heat turned up.

'Depussy's *Concerto for Recorder and Triangle* in four movements,' responded Gladys, as if she were training to be a continuity announcer. 'It was one of father's favourites. We used to perform it for him on Sundays at the rectory after he'd delivered his sermon. He said he found it calming after the rigours of his week.'

Tilly stifled a giggle as a vision of the Mulch sisters' Sunday recital on recorder and triangle came into her head. 'When was the last time you saw or spoke to Miss Jingle?' asked Hettie, pushing on with her questions.

The two sisters looked at each other as if deciding what to say next. This time, Dahlia spoke. 'Yesterday afternoon. She called to us over the hedge, which was strange as we hadn't spoken to her since last Michaelmas on account of the earwig situation. She was a bit upset. She said she'd had a detective asking questions. I suppose that must have been you.'

Hettie nodded, and Gladys continued, 'She told us she thought we should all be careful of what we said in these strange times. She was worried about Micks and how the murder might affect him, and said that no good could come of strangers visiting the plots.'

'Why do you think she was so worried about Micks?' Hettie asked.

'Those two were as thick as thieves,' said Dahlia, with a slight hint of contempt. 'He was always round there, and she encouraged him with his silly plays and helped him learn his lines. One day last week they were practising a sword fight on her veranda. She looked ridiculous in her long dressing gown, and he was done up like something from *Robin Hood*. He's a child, really, and Gertrude mothered him.'

'And what about strangers visiting the plots? What did she mean by that?'

'I suppose she meant the body on Bonny Grubb's patch, but I'm not sure. You could never have an ordinary chat with Gertrude. She was a bit like a bumblebee, just flitting from one subject to another. Not that I want to speak ill of the dead, but she was definitely out with the fairies most of the time. I think that's why she spent so much time with Micks. Cats of a feather flock together.'

Hettie smiled, recalling her encounter with Gertrude Jingle. 'Is that all she had to say to you?'

'Yes,' said Gladys. 'Blackberry arrived to collect some lilies for Malkin and Sprinkle, so she went off to deal with her.'

'And did Miss Jingle have any other visitors yesterday?'

'I think I heard Apple talking to her shortly after Blackberry left,' said Dahlia. 'I was in and out because of the rain, but I did see Desiree Chit later on the path. She'd taken Gertrude a slice of cake for her supper, and Micks was there around teatime.'

'What about later?' asked Hettie. 'Or even very early this morning? Any noises or disturbance?'

The Mulch sisters shook their heads in unison. It seemed that there were a number of comings and goings on Gertrude Jingle's allotment the day before, but nothing in any way significant to the carnage that Hettie had encountered that morning. The attack had been vicious and violent, and as Hettie studied the two sisters, she found it hard to believe that either of them was capable of anything more than a fatal poisoning or a nice pillow smothering while the victim was asleep. In her book, they weren't quite off the hook, but they had certainly slid down the suspect list.

Her assessment of the Mulches was rudely interrupted by a bout of expletives coming from Gertrude Jingle's plot. As all four cats moved to the boundary hedge, the substantial figure of Morbid Balm, the town's mortician, loomed up at them from the other side of the hedge.

The attractive black and white Goth cat was renowned for her artistic qualities regarding the dead. It was with great pride and job satisfaction that she went about her work, sending deceased cats on their final journeys looking the very best that they could under the circumstances. Morbid had performed several miracles at the town's literary festival earlier that summer, and Hettie and Tilly would be for ever grateful to her; at the time, they had been up to their tabby necks in a rather gruesome set of murders.

'Oh, it's you,' said Morbid, looking at Hettie and Tilly. 'Miss Wither-Fork said she'd called some detectives in. Bit of a mess this one, I gather. Wants an outdoor cremation – makes a nice change, but I can't get into the summer house. The key I picked up from the gatehouse doesn't seem to work. Miss Wither-Fork said she'd leave it there with her sister.'

At that moment, Mash Wither-Spoon appeared at Gertrude's gate. 'I'm so sorry, Miss Balm – I've given you the key to our shed by mistake. This is the one you need.' Mash made her way onto Gertrude Jingle's plot, swiftly followed by Hettie and Tilly. They left the Mulch sisters staring over the hedge, fascinated by the prospect of an outdoor funeral and keen to watch the preparations.

Exchanging keys with Mash, Morbid returned to the summer house and unlocked the door. Hettie was already aware of what lay behind it, and Tilly stood back, preferring to view the crime scene from a respectful distance. Mash Wither-Spoon moved forward, her curiosity getting the better of her. A blood-curdling scream of anguish came from somewhere very deep inside as she saw the true horror of the scene through the open door. She stared for a moment, taking in every gory detail, then threw her paws up to her eyes to block out the vision, staggering backwards and collapsing in a sobbing heap on the herringbone brick path. Tilly attempted to console her, but the sobs became louder and more frequent, punctuated by the occasional 'Why?' and 'How could this happen?' – both questions that Hettie and Tilly would have loved to know the answers to.

Morbid was seemingly unmoved by the body and its surrounding chaos, but she took several minutes to process what was in front of her. Eventually, she turned to Hettie, having sized up the task before her. 'I could do with a bit of help on this one,' she said, raising her voice above the continuous wailing. Hettie signalled to Tilly to coax Mash back to the gatehouse, and she and Morbid moved into the summer house to prepare Gertrude Jingle for her ongoing journey.

Morbid cleared a space on the table and set down her small suitcase, which contained all the tools of her trade. She opened the catches and the lid popped up to reveal a set of drawers, all neatly labelled and containing eyes, ears, whiskers and even tails. The rest of the suitcase was laid out with brushes, combs, shampoo, cotton wool and a parcel of sandwiches, which Morbid removed first and put to one side. 'Got the call as I was about to eat my lunch,' she said, unwrapping the parcel and taking a healthy bite. 'We need to get her cleaned up first. A pan of hot water would be good for starters.'

While Morbid worked her way through the tuna sandwiches, Hettie scrambled some sticks together and lit the small stove. Filling the kettle from one of the clean water butts in the garden, she set it to boil on the stove as Morbid turned to the body. 'We'll need something to dress her in. Maybe you could find a clean nightdress or something?'

Hettie looked round the small hut. There was nothing to suggest a clothes store of any kind, but she noticed that the bed itself had drawers below the mattress. The first was full of papers, letters and an assortment of old photographs, but the second contained what she was looking for: on top of a pile of fresh laundry was a white nightdress, a far cry from the bloodied garment in which Gertrude Jingle was currently displayed. She watched as Morbid gently removed first the bed sheet and then the nightdress from the body. The fur was matted with congealed blood around the entry wounds, where the killer's knife had done its work. Undaunted, Morbid filled a bowl with warm water and bathed the injuries as if Gertrude were still alive. The care and attention she gave to the body as she went about her work left Hettie in tears, bathing away the horror and brushing the fur back over the wounds to restore some dignity to the cat who – in life – had been a proud and genteel member of the allotment community.

Not wishing to get in the way, Hettie busied herself by gathering the lilies that had littered the floor and the bed. Remembering that they were to be consumed in the funeral fire, she piled them up outside the hut. There was a click of the gate and she looked up to see Rooster Chit coming up the path, carrying a fork and spade in his paws. 'Miss Wither-Fork wants me to lift Miss Jingle's bulbs,' he said. 'It's a sad day, that it is. I can't believe she's gone. My Desiree brought 'er a nice bit of cake up for 'er tea only yesterday. Said she was singing to 'er flowers in the rain, 'appy as a seagull on an open fish box.'

Hettie admired Rooster Chit's analogy, but blocked his way as he attempted to peer into the summer house. 'Miss Jingle is being prepared for her funeral,' she said, diverting his attention from the hut to the spade and fork in his paws. 'It's going to be an outdoor cremation and all the lilies are to be burnt with her.'

'Right-o,' he said. 'I'd better get on, then.' Rooster retraced his footsteps and began the sad task of lifting the lily bulbs one by one. Hettie looked on as Gertrude Jingle's beautiful family was uprooted and piled up in a mountain of snowy-white flowers, still clinging to their bulbs, so recently wrenched from the earth. Their scent filled the air, and the bees swarmed in anger as their pollen supply was disturbed with such finality.

When she returned to the summer house, she was amazed by the transformation that Morbid had achieved in such a short time. A pile of bloodied sheets lay in a heap on the floor, replaced by the fresh, clean ones that Morbid had mined from the drawer. Miss Jingle was at peace in her bed, with no sign of the violence that had befallen her only a few hours ago. 'You've worked a miracle,' said Hettie in admiration.

'All part of the service.' Morbid snapped the catches shut on her case. 'Although the sooner you get your paws on the killer, the better we'll like it. Nasty business. She's been treated like a pincushion, and with some force – a lot of anger there. I reckon she was alive for most of it, judging by the amount of blood. I found this by her pillow – she'd been gagged to keep her quiet, but obviously the killer removed it when he'd finished his work.'

Hettie stared down at the handkerchief, still knotted and – like everything else – stained with Miss Jingle's blood. 'So she was tortured?'

'Yep, looks like it,' said Morbid. 'Not at all like the one we picked up from here yesterday. One good blow to the head did for him, and a couple more to make sure of the job – that's when the teeth came out. Nothing like this, though.'

Hettie thought for a moment, grateful for Morbid's observations. 'Do you think there could be two murderers, then?' she asked, considering a breakthrough that she really didn't need.

Morbid put her head on one side and thought about it. 'Well, professionally I'd have to say that the deaths couldn't be further apart. This one has been set up to look as staged as possible. It's almost artistic with the lilies and all that. The other one was a hit-and-run sort of thing, with none of the violence we've seen here.'

Hettie stared at the body laid out on the bed and marvelled at how peaceful Miss Jingle looked in the surrounding bloody chaos of the hut. She picked the broken glasses up from the floor, together with the book that lay by them; the blood had soaked through the pages and was now dry enough for her to take a closer look, and she saw that it was a copy of *Macbeth*.

'That's it for now,' said Morbid, picking up her case. 'I'll be back here nice and early tomorrow, as the hut will have to come down. We'll have to use it to build a pyre, so it's all paws on deck for that. I've only seen it done once, when I was visiting an Indian cat friend of mine who lived at the foot of the Himalayas. He saw his mother off in an outdoor cremation. Lovely, it was, all very colourful and much nicer than the ovens up the crem – a chance to say a proper goodbye. It's all about the spirit leaving the body so it can be reincarnated. According to custom, the old worn-out body has to be burnt to be reborn. I thought at the time that it was a really cool thing to do, but I never thought I'd be organising one. Can't see it catching on at Shroud and Trestle.'

Hettie liked Morbid Balm. Dressed in her short black tunic and tights, finished off with a pair of black Doc Martens boots and adorned with silver jewellery, pierced ears, a ring through her nose, and a giant cross of black ebony round her neck, she looked as far away from her chosen profession as she could be. No sombre understated suit and fixed expression of sympathy for her; just a smile that lit up even the worst of feline catastrophes, and a willingness to restore order and beauty for the dead as well as the living.

'Are you going to burn everything at the funeral?' asked Hettie, getting back to practicalities.

'Yep. Miss Wither-Fork says the whole lot's got to go up in flames in accordance with the deceased's wishes – a sort of purification, I suppose. Those lilies will make a great decoration for the body, and I'll try to get all her stuff underneath her. Should go up a treat.'

Hettie looked across at the bed and the open drawer

of papers. 'It would really help if I could borrow those papers overnight,' she said, looking slightly shifty. 'There may be some clues as to why she was murdered.'

'Gotcha thinking,' responded Morbid with a wink. 'If you have them back here by mid morning tomorrow, I don't think anyone would notice. And who's going to argue, anyway?'

Hettie gave a conspiratorial nod as Tilly arrived at the hut door, relieved to see that Gertrude Jingle was now at rest.

'Perfect timing,' said Hettie. 'Help me gather up these papers. We're borrowing them for a little light reading after supper.'

Tilly, while slightly reticent about approaching the body, noticed that there was a battered old suitcase at the bottom of the bed. She dragged it across the floor and discovered that there were more papers inside it. The two cats added the contents of the drawer and dragged the suitcase out into the sunshine, leaving Morbid to lock up. She gave them a cheery goodbye and set off down the allotment path, while they contemplated their next move.

'How was Mash when you left her?' Hettie asked, as they sat on Gertrude's veranda and watched Rooster Chit demolish the garden.

'Sobbing and wringing her paws. There was no consoling her, and she was almost hysterical. She just kept asking how this could have happened. I suppose she was quite close to Miss Jingle, what with the plays and all that stuff.'

'Was there any sign of Micks while you were there?'

'No, but I assumed he was still upstairs in his turret room. He must have heard the noise Mash was making, but maybe he thought she was practising her Lady Macbeth – the bit where she's trying to get the blood off her paws.'

'This whole business gets more like a bloody Shakespearian tragedy by the minute,' said Hettie, rubbing her eyes and wishing she'd brought her sunglasses; the headache that had been threatening was starting to become a reality. 'Let's check out the knife with Bonny and have a quick word with Apple Chutney, then I think we'd better head for home and sift through this lot.'

Tilly picked up the sack containing the knife and the chutneys, and Hettie took charge of Miss Jingle's suitcase. The two friends nodded a goodbye to Rooster and made their way up the path to Bonny Grubb's allotment.

CHAPTER SEVENTEEN

Bonny Grubb awoke with a start at the sound of her gate being opened. She yawned and stretched, then licked one of her paws and gave her face and ears a cursory wash, noticing that she had visitors. 'What's up now?' she asked. 'No more of them murders, I hope. Mind you, at least old Gertrude kept to 'er own patch ta pop 'er clogs. I don't reckon me onions will ever recover.'

Hettie put the suitcase down and took the sack from Tilly, drawing out the knife. Bonny's eyes grew large as she stared at the murder weapon. 'Is that what done fer 'er?'

'I'm afraid it is, Bonny, and we need your help.

Have you seen this knife before?' Hettie handed it over, and Bonny turned it in her paw before giving her answer.

'It's one of me sharpenings,' she said. 'See, I always pushes *away* from the blade with me stone. Look – you can see me marks, nice an' sharp still. Cut through leather, that would.'

'And can you remember who it belongs to?' asked Hettie, holding her breath.

Bonny looked from Hettie to Tilly, then down at her gardening boots. 'I don't think I can say. I don't need no trouble. I've set me roots down 'ere an' I stay out of any business that might bring me harm. I only tell me own tales. I don't tell on others. Too dangerous.'

Hettie stared at the dejected and frightened Gypsy cat. She was beginning to tire of the lack of straight answers in the case, so adopted the same tactics that she'd used on the Mulch sisters earlier. 'Right, Bonny, you're obviously hiding something. Let me remind you that the body of the stranger was found on your patch, which puts you right up there with the main suspects. You also rifled through his pockets and stole things from him. If you don't tell me who owns this knife, I will have to assume that you're involved in the murders and are attempting to cover something up. So let's have it -- who does this knife belong to?'

Bonny made a failed attempt to block out Hettie's words by putting her paws up to her ears, visibly rattled by the accusations that had been flung at her. 'Stop!' she cried. 'You don't understand. 'E'll run me off me patch if I tell. 'E did for them cats in Southwool. Set fire to 'em, 'e did. I shan't sleep for 'im burnin' me caravan down while I'm in it.'

Hettie had the answer she needed. 'That's fine, Bonny. No need to give me a name, and don't worry – I won't betray you. Before we leave, are you sure there's nothing else you can tell us about Miss Jingle or the dead stranger?'

Relieved to be off Hettie's hook, Bonny thought hard about the question. 'There *is* one thing,' she said, 'but that don't seem important.' Hettie urged Bonny to continue, this time coaxing her gently. 'Well, it's Ruben Grubb, as I calls 'im. 'E was in me brassicas patch last Sunday morning, and then 'e was gone. I thought 'e was me best chance at a prize this year, but 'e just upped and left, stick an' all.'

Hettie was confused, but Tilly came to the rescue. 'Was Ruben Grubb a scarecrow?'

''E was more than that to me,' said Bonny. ''E was the spit of an old Gypsy tom I fell for a few years back. I 'ad an old picture of 'im an' I showed it to Blackberry – she made 'im up for me for the show. I'm not sure when 'e took off, what with the murder and everything, but I seen 'e wasn't there this morning when I went to lift some cabbages for the show. Tha's the trouble with them Gypsy toms – loves yer and leaves yer, off on the open road before the day breaks.'

Hettie had enough on her paws without a missing scarecrow, and now she would have to find a way of confronting Jeremiah Corbit about the knife whilst keeping Bonny out of the firing line. Leaving her to resume her sunbathing, she and Tilly stepped back onto the path and almost ran into Apple Chutney, who was wheeling a trolley stacked with jars of every colour and size imaginable. 'Whoops!' she said. 'I'm sorry, I didn't see you. I'm taking this lot up to the Hall. I've got to do a drop-off at the church for the harvest festival, and the rest of them are going on me stall. Just the damson and lime marmalade to bottle up and I'm done.'

Hettie decided to interrupt the flow of preserves for fear that the afternoon would slip away from them on a tide of pickled fruit and vegetables. 'I wonder if you have a minute to clear something up?' she began. Apple looked slightly wary, but nodded. 'I understand that you visited Miss Jingle yesterday afternoon?'

'No, I didn't. I was in me chutney shed most of the day, and I didn't go down that end at all. Why? Who said I did? I suppose it was Corbit, was it?'

Hettie shook her head. 'No, it was the Mulch

sisters. They seemed to think they heard you talking to Miss Jingle yesterday.'

Apple looked put out and more than a little cross, but obviously felt the need to clarify the situation. 'I haven't spoken to Miss Jingle for a week. The last time I saw her was when I went looking for me scarecrow. I'd left it in me bean plot. Lovely, it was – a real winner. A great pumpkin head on it and dressed like a French cat with a beret and striped top. I even made a string of shallots to go round his neck. I got up one morning and he was gone. I hardly dare tell Blackberry – she spent such a lot of time making it for me. Miss Jingle said hers had gone missing as well, but she didn't seem that bothered about it. She was too busy with her lilies, getting them ready for the show. As for the Mulches, they only hear what they want to hear. I definitely didn't see or speak to Miss Jingle yesterday.'

Hettie believed what Apple was telling her, although it threw up yet another mystery: if it wasn't Apple Chutney, who had the Mulches heard? Or were they deliberately trying to confuse? In any event, Jeremiah Corbit was next on Hettie's list, and that confrontation was seconds away.

Apple Chutney clinked and rattled her way to the gatehouse with the fruits of her labours, while Hettie and Tilly headed for the compost heaps. Even on a sunny day, Corbit's allotment looked grim and unwelcoming. Putting the suitcase down at the gate and pulling the knife out of the sack, Hettie lifted the latch and left Tilly to guard the papers and chutneys. For a moment, she thought she was out of luck: there was no sign of Corbit, and she was about to turn on her heel when his voice rang out from behind the shed. 'Are you looking for me?' he called, emerging with a wheelbarrow full of rotting lilies.

Hettie looked at the barrow and then at Corbit before pointing the knife in his direction. 'I believe this is yours, Mr Corbit. I found it during the process of my enquiries.'

Corbit came forward and studied the knife at close range before responding. 'It certainly looks like mine. Where did you find it?'

'Hidden in a bloody handkerchief in Miss Jingle's greenhouse,' said Hettie, watching his reaction very closely.

There *was* no reaction to speak of. Corbit just shrugged his bony shoulders and carried on wheeling his barrow over to one of the steaming stacks of compost, where he forked the lilies onto the heap.

'Did those lilies come from Miss Jingle's?' she asked, trying to engage him again.

Corbit turned to her. This time there was anger in his face, and the grizzly grey hackles rose on the back of his neck. 'For a detective, you seem a little short on questions. Why don't you just ask me if I murdered

Gertrude Jingle and have done with it, instead of beating about the bush? That way we can all get on without any more pointless interruptions.'

Hettie was taken aback at his directness and found herself doing as he'd asked. 'Did you murder Gertrude Jingle?'

Corbit spat into the compost heap and pulled a pipe from his pocket, along with a tobacco pouch. He took his time filling it, as Hettie stood waiting for an answer. Eventually, in the cloud of acrid smoke that billowed from the pipe, he spoke. 'No, I didn't kill Gertrude Jingle. That knife has been missing for days. In fact, the last time I saw it was on Miss Jingle's plot, where I used it to cut down the lilies that had gone over. I did that for her on a regular basis, and she let me have the dead flowers for composting. These lilies here were the ones I cut down, and they've been rotting down for several days behind my shed. Now, if you've nothing else to say, I suggest you return my knife to me, collect your little friend from my gate, and go and bother someone else.'

Corbit held out his paw, waiting for Hettie to hand over the knife. She faltered briefly, but withdrew it at the last moment, refusing to be intimidated. 'I'm afraid the knife is evidence, and until Miss Jingle's killer is revealed it stays with me. My "little friend" and I will continue our investigations. I'm most grateful for your help and the gracious way you've answered my questions. I can see now why you're so popular up here on the allotments. Your charm and personality must be a real asset.'

Like most bullies, Jeremiah Corbit was flawed by Hettie's sarcasm. It left him with nothing to say, and he slunk back into his lonely world of decomposing flowers and vegetables. Hettie closed the gate behind her, and she and Tilly set out for Wither-Fork Hill, hoping for a bus to take them home. They stood opposite the gatehouse for some time, waiting for a lift that clearly wasn't coming, but it gave Hettie the chance to study Micks Wither-Spoon's turret at close range. Gertrude was right: he had a perfect view of the bottom end of the allotments, and she was concerned about not having spoken to him directly. There was no sign of him on his battlements and her gaze fell to the side of the gatehouse, where a motorbike stood half-covered in a plastic sheet. As she watched, Micks appeared from the backyard, pulled the plastic sheet away and wheeled the motorbike out onto the road. He kicked the machine into life before she could stop him, then sped off into the countryside in a cloud of smoke, giving full throttle to the engine as he roared away into the distance.

Hettie swore under her breath, knowing she'd missed her chance, but minutes later the sound of a motorbike engine returned, and this time Tilly screamed with delight. The noise came from the bottom of Wither-Fork Hill, and Tilly clapped her paws with joy as she recognised the beautifully tuned engine of Miss Scarlet, their official and much-loved mode of transport. The motorbike and sidecar was driven by their friend, Bruiser, who had become an integral part of the No. 2 Feline Detective Agency. He brought it to a skidding halt in front of them, and Hettie and Tilly beamed at him. 'I thought you were on holiday until the weekend?' said Hettie, loading Tilly, the suitcase, the knife and the chutneys into the sidecar.

'I was missin' me shed,' shouted Bruiser over the roar of the engine. 'And I 'ad a feelin' that I might be needed, so I came back early. The Butters said you was stuck up 'ere on a murder case.'

Hettie leapt onto the motorbike behind Bruiser and the three friends roared off into town. They were soon catching up on their news, helped by a selection of savoury pastries that Betty and Beryl had put aside as a welcome back for Bruiser's afternoon tea. The Butters had adopted Bruiser and welcomed him into their protective world, gifting him a shed at the bottom of their garden and making him their lad about the yard. He'd roamed the highways and byways for many years, living under the stars and never staying long in any one place, but now – as age made a warm bed and a roof over his head more enticing – he had quickly settled into the first proper home he'd had since leaving his birthplace to seek his fortune. He finally found that fortune when he paid a visit to Hettie one cold winter's night; within days, Hettie and Tilly had enlisted him as driver and chief muscle in their detective agency, and he had been a vital part in the solving of several high-profile cases. Hettie would be the first to agree that on a number of occasions he had saved their long-haired tabby necks.

There was a message waiting for them on the answering machine from Fluff Wither-Fork, confirming that Miss Jingle's cremation would begin at midday and that there would be no particular dress code. Tilly was relieved, as black had never suited her, and Hettie wasn't bothered one way or the other. The good news was that the Chits had agreed to supply wake bakes; both Hettie and Tilly were delighted with this news, and looked forward to more of Desiree's potato cakes.

Hettie did her best to outline The Michaelmas Murders case to Bruiser, who sat quietly taking in all the details. On hearing of the impending cremation, he instantly offered his services to Morbid with some of the heavier work that would be needed to prepare the pyre. He seemed pleased to have another case to get his teeth into, and went off happily to his shed with a Butters' steak and ale pie for supper, promising to have Miss

Scarlet ready for action at nine o'clock the following morning. It would be some time before Hettie and Tilly put themselves to bed, as Miss Jingle's papers were to prove much more interesting than expected.

CHAPTER EIGHTEEN

The September sun had excelled itself with such a beautiful warm day, but there was a definite nip in the air as Hettie staggered in under the weight of the coal scuttle, which she'd filled from a stack in the Butters' backyard. 'Let's get the fire lit and settle down with Miss Jingle's papers,' she said, as Tilly laid sticks and rolled up newspaper in the grate. 'I think we can wait a bit for our supper. It'll give us something to look forward to later.'

Tilly agreed, glancing up at the staff sideboard where a bag contained two sausage, liver and bacon pies. She put a match to the coals, and soon a healthy set of flames leapt up the chimney, bringing warmth to their room.

Hettie kicked off her day clothes and wrapped herself in her dressing gown; Tilly did the same, choosing a pair of pink and purple striped pyjamas. The pyjamas had originally been white with purple stripes, but Tilly had had a slight misunderstanding with one of Hettie's red T-shirts in the Butters' new twin-tub before going on holiday. She approached the age of mod cons with great trepidation, much preferring her tried-and-tested method of a tin bath in the backyard – not that she believed in washing anything too often. As far as the pyjamas were concerned, she was making the best of a bad job and had grown to love the added pink tinge to her nightwear – and anyway, the only cat who would see her wearing them was Hettie, who noticed very little when it came to clothes and colour coordination.

Hettie tipped the contents of the suitcase out onto the hearthrug, and Tilly made two piles: one of photographs; the other of letters and what looked to be official documents. She stared down at the papers and had one of her sad moments. 'It looks like there's a whole life here,' she said. 'Not much to show for a cat who once had everything.'

'She seemed happy enough dancing round her flowers,' said Hettie, picking up a bunch of letters tied with red ribbon and sniffing them before trying to decipher the writing. 'Sometimes wealth brings too many responsibilities. Look at Fluff Wither-Fork. I bet she'd rather be left alone to talk to her flowers and fountains.' She pulled the bundle of letters closer to her and squinted at the top one, trying to make sense of it. 'I hope it's not all going to be this hard to read,' she added, passing it to Tilly. 'What do you make of these?'

Tilly did as Hettie had done and sniffed the letters first. 'That's a lovely smell. It's like those perfume sticks that Jessie lights in her back room at the charity shop.'

'Joss sticks?' offered Hettie.

'Yes, and you can't read these letters because they're foreign. Indian, I think. Definitely not Chinese, because they write up and down.'

'Well, that's just brilliant!' said Hettie, getting more annoyed by the second. 'We've got hardly any time to go through this lot before it all goes up in smoke, and we've got a bloody language barrier on our paws!'

Tilly giggled at Hettie's outburst. She knew her friend was tired and that their day was turning out to be much longer than planned, but the work had to be got through and the quicker the better. 'Let's look at the photos first. That's a nice job. I think we should ignore the letters.'

Hettie nodded in agreement and tossed the bundle of letters back into the suitcase with a certain amount of bad grace. Many of the photographs were old and yellowing, but Miss Jingle had scribbled on the back of most of them, which proved to be a real help to Hettie and Tilly as they sat by the fire dismantling her life. The first batch that Tilly chose looked the oldest and showed groups of cats all dressed in their Sunday best, staring diligently at the camera. The same four cats appeared in a whole group of photos seemingly taken at the same time – a male and a female adult cat and two much smaller females, suggesting a family gathering. Tilly turned several of them over and was dismayed to find nothing written on the back until almost the last in the series. There it was: 'Mother, Father, Scoop and me', scrawled across the back in red ink.

'That's a start,' said Tilly brightly. 'It looks like Miss Jingle had a sister, and here's one of her parents again – on their own this time. She's written "Ma and Pa Jingle" on the back.'

'Well, I don't see how any of that helps,' said Hettie. 'Anything more recent?'

Tilly put aside the family photos and picked out another picture at random. It was a wedding photograph, and showed the bride and groom smiling in a church doorway. This time the writing on the back proved a little more helpful. '"Scoop and Lorrie Wither-Spoon on their wedding day",' said Tilly, emphasising the Wither-Spoon for Hettie's benefit.

Hettie snatched the photograph from Tilly's paw, suddenly focused on the job again. 'So Micks Wither-Spoon must somehow be related to Gertrude Jingle!'

'Looks like it,' said Tilly, getting excited, 'and here's a good one – the same cats but with a kitten! It says "Scoop, Lorrie and Micks"! If they're Micks' parents, then they must be the ones who were stabbed in the dressing room that Fluff told us about.'

'Which means that Micks Wither-Spoon is Gertrude Jingle's nephew!' said Hettie, looking confused. 'But according to Clippy Lean the nephew bankrupted Miss Jingle's estate and left her penniless. That can't be right, and Miss Jingle didn't talk to me about Micks as if they were related, either. See if you can turn up any pictures of Miss Jingle later in her life. We can try and pin down what happened to make her so poor. Nothing is adding up so far.'

Tilly sifted through more photos, hoping to come across a grand mansion with tea parties on the lawn, but nothing presented itself. Hettie returned to the pile of papers, not really knowing what she was looking for. She found the land document signed by Fluff Wither-Fork giving Gertrude rights to her allotment, and receipts for countless exotic-sounding bulbs and shrubs. There were a number of folded theatre posters heralding performances by Scoop and Lorrie Wither-Spoon; one of them even mentioned the introduction of 'The Infant Micks', as he was billed.

'I can see where Micks gets his dramatic tendencies from, and why Miss Jingle was so encouraging towards Micks' and Mash's little productions,' said Hettie.

'But are we to assume that Micks doesn't know he's related to her? And if he *does* know, could he be our killer? Maybe they had a row. Mash said Miss Jingle could be harsh with him, so perhaps it turned nasty.'

Their hearthrug was now covered in a mountain of photographs and papers, and Hettie and Tilly – energised by their discoveries – lost all notion of time. The pies and tarts sat undisturbed on the staff sideboard as the two cats plundered Gertrude Jingle's long life. Hettie turned up a cache of newspaper cuttings, lurid in their description of Scoop and Lorrie Wither-Spoon's murder. The facts were the same as Fluff had outlined, and one of the newspapers reported that the couple's young son had been taken into care by a local kitten charity. 'That's odd,' said Hettie, reading the report again. 'I wonder why Miss Jingle didn't take Micks on instead of letting him be raised as an orphan? She obviously took an interest in him, and she didn't seem the sort to walk away from a problem.'

'But she obviously did,' Tilly pointed out. 'When she lost her house, she walked away and set up on Wither-Fork allotments with nothing more than a few lily bulbs and a shed. Maybe she wanted to spend her final years close to Micks because she felt guilty for not looking after him when her sister died. Perhaps she didn't tell him who she was because she felt ashamed of how she'd behaved.'

Hettie had to agree that Tilly had come up with

the best explanation yet, but there was still no sign of Gertrude Jingle's life between the death of her sister and her arrival at Wither-Fork. She gathered some of the papers and photographs they'd already been through and put them back in the suitcase; as she did so, she noticed that the case had an extra pouch in the lid, held in place by a strap and buckle. The buckle was rusted with age and the strap came away in Hettie's paws. Inside the pouch was an elaborately jewelled and embroidered satin clutch bag. Hettie pounced on it as Tilly added more coal to their fire. The satin bag gave off the same heady smell that the bundle of letters had offered, and she placed it down in front of the fire and opened it. Out tumbled the missing years of Gertrude Jingle's life, along with a tiny ornamental pot.

Hettie put the small pot to one side, and Tilly began to look through the photographs inside the bag. 'I think Miss Jingle was one of those Bollywood cats. These photos are beautiful, and look at that handsome Indian cat with her – can you see the lovely stripes on his face? And here on the back – it says Maharaja Gadget Jodpurr and his bride Maharani Gertrude Jodpurr. They're standing in front of one of those white marbled palaces!' Tilly could hardly contain herself at the thought of Miss Jingle being a Bollywood movie star. She continued to sort through photographs, which showed the couple involved in various ceremonies, always smiling at the camera or at each other. There was also a picture of the marbled palace Tilly had admired; on the back, Gertrude had written 'Sheesh Mahal' and in brackets 'The Palace of Mirrors'. 'Oh, she looks so lovely in her costumes. I wonder if we could get hold of the film she was making?'

'She wasn't making a film,' said Hettie, bringing Tilly back down to earth with a bump. 'Look at these newspaper cuttings. She was actually married to a maharaja. According to this, she met him on a cruise round the Greek Islands – it was a whirlwind romance and he whisked her off to his palace in Rishikesh in India. It says he was one of the last true maharajas, and she became Rajmata Jodpurr after his death. Apparently, Rajmata means a widow of an Indian prince. Evidently, she disappeared after his funeral. They were together for eight years until a bunch of marbled cats led by Deepak Rishabh attacked their palace, Sheesh Mahal, and stabbed him to death. The marbled cats are described here as "a wild and lawless band of cut-throats". They took her prisoner, but she was allowed to attend his cremation and obviously hooked off while no one was watching. And look, this cutting has a picture of the funeral. He's being cremated outside in the open air on the banks of the river. And there she is, watching him go up in smoke.'

'So that's why she's chosen such an odd funeral,' said Tilly. 'And that's why she didn't help Micks – she was thousands of miles away, having a happy life with her Indian prince.'

'Exactly!' said Hettie. 'And her story about falling on hard times was almost accurate – if you discount the fact that she was the wife of an Indian prince living in a grand palace bedecked with jewels, and run off the homestead by a bunch of cat thugs. You're right, of course – a story like this belongs in the realms of Bollywood. You've got to admire her for keeping all this under her bonnet, but we're still no closer to finding our murderer.'

'We might be,' said Tilly. 'What if the stranger was an Indian agent who came looking for her, and she bashed his head in and he had an accomplice who murdered her and escaped back to India.'

Hettie decided that there was much thinking to be done. Tilly's scenario was probably the best one yet, but she felt that the answer lay much closer to home, possibly in the gatehouse that guarded the Wither-Fork estate. 'Well, we've come on leaps and bounds,' she said. 'So now I suggest we catch up with those two pies and the custard tarts before they end up being breakfast.'

CHAPTER NINETEEN

The revelations of Gertrude Jingle's life kept Hettie awake long into the night. Tilly slept deeply in a dream world of exotic palaces, giant elephants, and the occasional jar of chutney being shared by a group of scarecrows. Both cats were expressing their muddled thoughts and neither was able to face the new day with any clarity. Due to her lack of sleep, Hettie awoke with one of her heads. The noise of Tilly scrabbling about in the bottom drawer of their filing cabinet, looking for something appropriate to wear for the funeral, didn't help – and she said so.

Realising that Hettie was awake, bad-tempered and decidedly fractious, Tilly skipped to the kettle to make their morning tea and put two slices of bread in their pop-up toaster, which rarely popped up and always had to be interrupted during the creation of a burnt offering. Tilly was used to Hettie's moods, and circumvented them with her cheerful approach to each day. Food had always been a reliable cure for her friend's ill humour and today was no exception. Tilly delivered a milky tea and a slice of toast spread thickly with a cheese triangle to Hettie's armchair, where she slept in a tangle of dressing gown and blankets. Within minutes, Hettie was almost ready to face her day, and Tilly demolished her own breakfast and returned to the filing cabinet.

Hettie stretched and cleaned the cheese and toast crumbs from her whiskers. The clock on the staff sideboard said half past eight, and she yawned at the prospect of another long day up on the Wither-Fork allotments. 'I suppose we'd better get a move on,' she said, more to herself than to Tilly, who was now *in* the drawer of the filing cabinet, obscured by a heaving bundle of cardigans, T-shirts and coloured socks.

'At least it's going to be exciting,' Tilly said as she finally surfaced. 'I've never been to an outdoor cremation.'

'I don't suppose it's much different from a barbecue,' said Hettie, still erring on the side of grumpy. 'But we'll get a chance to observe everyone else while it's happening. I imagine it'll be a good turnout, and I'm particularly keen to watch the Wither-Spoons' reaction to it all.'

The day was set fair, and by the time Bruiser had parked Miss Scarlet outside the gatehouse the sun was already offering some late-summer warmth. Hettie and Tilly were pleased they'd gone for a light and colourful look to their clothes, especially as things would be hotting up on Miss Jingle's plot once Morbid got the cremation underway. Hettie glanced at the gatehouse and noticed that the motorbike Micks had been riding was no longer there. Her first thought was that he'd stayed away from home, but, as Bruiser took charge of the suitcase from Miss Scarlet's sidecar, Micks appeared on his battlements. 'You can't park that there,' he said. 'Not without permission.'

Hettie glanced up and noticed that Micks was dressed completely in black; as he leant out over his turret, he resembled a rather large crow. He began pacing the battlements, climbing up and down on them and teetering on the edge as if he were about to fly. Looking into his face, she could see a wildness in his eyes, as if he had lost all sense of danger. She, Bruiser and Tilly stood very still, their eyes trained on the demented cat, all holding their breath as the death-defying antics continued.

'Get down from there at once!' came a voice of reason, and Mash appeared, pulling Micks away from the edge. 'I've told you we have to behave today or

Fluff will ban us from the funeral – and you don't want to miss that, do you? Now, go in and finish your breakfast, and leave the folk down there to get on with their business.'

Micks disappeared and Mash offered her apologies to Hettie. 'Sorry about that. He's overexcited about all the cats coming and going. What with the show and now Miss Jingle's funeral, it's too much for him. As I told you the other day, he's too sensitive for his own good.'

'More like completely off his bloody head!' said Hettie, muttering so that only Tilly and Bruiser could hear. 'Come on – let's go and give Morbid some help. She'll need the suitcase. It's got to go up with the rest of Gertrude Jingle's stuff.'

The three friends turned their backs on Mash Wither-Spoon without another word and made their way to what had now become a funeral site. It was a hive of activity. Fluff Wither-Fork was helping Blackberry Tibbs to set up trestle tables ready for the funeral teas. Rooster Chit and Jeremiah Corbit were poised on ladders, dismantling the roof on the summer house. Tarragon Trench was adding some colour to the proceedings by sitting cross-legged on top of a mountain of lily bulbs, chanting some sort of mantra, which clearly only he could understand, and Hettie smiled in the knowledge that Miss Jingle would have approved of her lilies being given their last rites in such a way.

Bruiser instinctively headed for the summer house to lend his strength to the other two cats, who were grateful for another pair of paws, as Morbid Balm directed proceedings from the centre of the plot that she'd chosen for the cremation. Hettie and Tilly reported to her with the suitcase, and Morbid received it with a conspiratorial wink. 'All burnables in here?' she asked.

Hettie nodded, then remembered the jewelled clutch bag and the small pot. 'I think you should have a look. There are some things that might not burn.'

Morbid snapped the case open and instantly pounced on the pot. 'Ah, I think I know what this is,' she said, giving the lid a twist and sniffing the contents. 'Yup – funeral ashes. Someone she was close to, I expect. I'll add these in once we get things underway.'

Hettie and Tilly shared a knowing look. Hettie was tempted to share Miss Jingle's colourful past with Morbid, but decided against it on the basis that Fluff Wither-Fork was paying for their time and ought to be the first to know. 'What can we do to help?' she asked, sidestepping the issue of who the ashes were.

'I think Mrs Chit could do with an extra pair of paws. She's putting on the funeral tea, and I'd like some help with the body. I need to get it bound up nicely and moved out of the hut before the walls come down.' Morbid looked anxiously over at the summer house, which seemed to be rapidly becoming a demolition site.

Hettie followed her gaze and responded with a plan. 'I'll help with Miss Jingle, and Tilly can help Mrs Chit with the tea.'

Tilly clapped her paws with delight at being given such a nice job and wasted no time in removing herself from the chaos of the funeral arrangements. She was still getting used to the idea of dead bodies. Although she and Hettie had encountered quite a few since they'd started their detective agency, it was the part of the work that she disliked most – and anyway, Hettie was so much better at that sort of thing. In spite of her advanced years, Tilly had started out as Hettie's office junior and had rapidly progressed to chief sidekick, complete with business mac and turned-up collar. Hettie still shielded her from the more visceral aspects of their cases, though, and for that Tilly would be for ever grateful.

She made her way to Desiree Chit's boathouse, and Hettie followed Morbid to the summer house just as Fluff Wither-Fork announced a tea break. It was perfect timing, as it gave Hettie and Morbid a moment to talk quietly without the added soundtrack of the hut coming down around their ears. Miss Jingle was as Morbid had left her the day before, but a little dustier: the breaking up of the walls around her had made their mark with a smudge here and a splinter of wood there. 'If we're going to get this right, we need to wrap her in a sheet from top to toe, knotting it at both ends,' said Morbid, assessing the job. 'We can slide her outside on the mattress like a stretcher, then put the whole thing on top of the pyre when it's built. If we leave her in here for much longer, we risk the walls caving in around her as they take the shed down.'

Under the careful guidance of the mortician, Hettie assisted as the body was gently encased in a clean white sheet from Miss Jingle's fresh laundry drawer. She then moved the few sticks of furniture to one side, and the two cats slid the body with the mattress onto the floor, ready for its final journey out into the sunshine. Hettie looked back at the bed, and could hardly believe what she was seeing. Now that the mattress had been removed, another of Gertrude Jingle's secrets was revealed. 'Good grief!' she said. 'Just look at that! Corbit was spot on. She really does have a fortune under her mattress.' She moved closer and found several large bundles of banknotes and a white envelope addressed to Fluff Wither-Fork. 'I'll go and fetch Miss Wither-Fork,' she said, stepping over the mattress and the body to get to the door. 'You'd better stand guard until I get back.'

Fluff was pouring tea from a giant teapot when Hettie reached her, filling several mugs for the workers as Blackberry stood by her side, issuing the added incentive of a custard cream to each cat. Waving away the tea but accepting a biscuit, Hettie drew Fluff to one side. 'Miss Balm and I need to show you something that Miss Jingle has left behind,' she explained, leading the way back to the summer house.

Fluff had so far avoided the body, leaving others to deal with the more macabre aspects of the morning, but now she had to step over it in a rather ungainly fashion to reach the bed. Her first response to the money was a good one. 'Where in heaven's name did all this come from?' she cried. 'There must be a small fortune here! I've never seen so much money.'

'There's an envelope addressed to you as well. Perhaps that might offer an explanation,' said Morbid, hoping to be included in the solving of the mystery.

Fluff wasted no time in slitting the envelope open with one of her elegantly painted claws. She pulled a letter from inside and read it out loud for the benefit of Hettie and Morbid, who hung on her every word.

My dear Miss Wither-Fork,
If you are reading this it means that I have come to the end of my life, and I wouldn't want to move on to my next incarnation without thanking you for your kindness in allowing me to live out my days on this plot of land that has become my salvation.

I have already asked of you that my body should be cremated on this site along with all my worldly goods and beautiful flowers, but there are other things that I would be most grateful if you could do for me in my absence from this life.

I fear for Micks Wither-Spoon, as he is a danger to himself, and your sister – though brave – may need your help to make a new life for herself one day. I would like you to take the money you find here and use it for the benefit of Wither-Fork Hall and Mash's future, should she need it, after my funeral costs have been deducted. I leave you as sole beneficiary to my estate, and ask that you spend or invest the money wisely.

I trust that you will make all the right decisions should the time come, and in the event of history repeating itself, that you will be there to pick up the pieces.

Please regard this letter as my last will and testament, and let us hope we meet again in another life.

Your grateful tenant. Peace always.

Rajmata Gertrude Jingle Jodpurr

Fluff Wither-Fork reread the letter several times to herself before addressing Hettie and Morbid, who stood patiently waiting for her response. 'I'm totally shocked. Gertrude always talked in riddles, but this letter is extreme. What can she mean about Micks and Mash? If ever there was a strong partnership, it's theirs. Why would Mash want a new life? The one she has is a little surreal at times, but I can't see her ever leaving Micks, and he certainly knows which side his bread is buttered –

he sticks to her like glue. And what about this signature? "Rajmata" and "Jodpurr" – what can all that be about?'

Morbid continued to look confused, not really understanding who Micks and Mash were and hoping for an explanation. Hettie was about to fill in the details when Jeremiah, Rooster and Bruiser returned from their tea break, armed with hammers and screwdrivers to complete the demolition of the summer house. Morbid moved swiftly into undertaker mode as Hettie threw one of Miss Jingle's sheets across the money on the bed to conceal it from prying eyes. 'You'll have to give us five minutes, gents,' Morbid said, helping Fluff across the mattress and into the sunshine. 'We need to get Miss Jingle out of the hut before you do any more to it. We're going to slide her out on her mattress.'

Jeremiah Corbit and Rooster Chit stood by as Bruiser and Morbid steered and tugged the mattress through the door with its precious cargo. All the assembled workers then bore Miss Jingle across the plot, bringing her to rest in the shade of the cherry tree that bordered the Mulch sisters' allotment. Hettie stayed behind in the hut, gathered up the money in the sheet and presented it to Fluff Wither-Fork, who was standing abandoned and bewildered next to the pile of lily bulbs, with only Tarragon Trench for company. 'I think you should return to Wither-Fork Hall with this,' she said. 'It would be safer there and it'll give you some time to come to terms with what's happened.'

'I'm most grateful for your concern, but I'm so confused by this letter. It feels like a warning of things to come, and all this money – I don't know whether to jump for joy or sink into despair. I understood that Miss Jingle was penniless, and why was she so involved with Micks and Mash?'

'I think I can answer some of those questions,' said Hettie. 'But not here. Shall I walk you back to the Hall? I'm sure Morbid can spare me for half an hour.'

Fluff nodded, and Hettie accompanied her to the gate, stopping off to let Morbid know the revised plans. There was no sign of Micks or Mash at the gatehouse, for which Hettie was grateful; the last thing she needed was another command performance from the Wither-Spoons. They had only got halfway across the parkland, though, before Mash bumped into them from the other direction. 'Oh, I wondered where you were,' she said. 'I'm afraid I've got some bad news. We have to withdraw our *Macbeth* from the show. Micks is a bag of nerves and now he's starting a cold. We just can't manage it.'

Under normal circumstances, Fluff would have danced a jig at the prospect of a no-show from the Wither-Spoons. Instead, she dismissed her sister with a single word, 'fine', and moved on with Hettie towards the Hall, leaving Mash to stare after her.

CHAPTER TWENTY

Tilly walked in on a real party atmosphere in Desiree Chit's boathouse. Bonny Grubb was sitting by the stove, playing her concertina for the benefit of Blight Chit, who danced and clapped his paws to the music. Apple Chutney was buttering a mountain of freshly baked bread baps, and Desiree was filling pastry cases with egg mixture, ready to bake off as savoury flans. 'Come in, my lovely,' she said as Tilly opened the door. 'What can I do for you?'

'I'm reporting for duty, if there's anything I can do to help?'

'Bless you! 'Ow do you feel about creamin' and jammin'?' asked Desiree, wiping her paws on her apron.

Tilly looked a little confused about what 'creamin''
and 'jammin'' might entail, but accepted the job
willingly as there was nothing nasty about Desiree Chit
or her boathouse. Apple Chutney obviously knew what
was coming, and made space on the table as Desiree
pulled a substantial batch of scones from her oven and
banged them down in front of Tilly. 'There you are!
Give 'em a minute or two to settle, then you can start
splittin' them and creamin' and jammin'. Lovely little
job for you. You'd better put this apron on, though –
things can get a bit messy, and you wouldn't want to
spoil your nice outfit, would you?'

Tilly clambered into the apron, which was much
too big for her, and Desiree added a large bowl of thick
clotted cream to the table. 'Now then, Apple – which
of your lovely jams shall we have for the job? I've got
strawberry, raspberry and damson. We ate the last of
your gooseberry preserve for breakfast this morning.
My Rooster can't keep his paws off the stuff.'

Apple stopped buttering her baps and put her
head on one side, as if weighing up the troubles of
the world. Tilly and Desiree waited in anticipation
for her decision, and even Bonny Grubb brought her
current tune to an abrupt conclusion, keen to know
the outcome. It was Blight Chit who eventually broke
the silence by shouting 'Strawberry!' at the top of his
squeaky little voice, defusing the tension and saving
Apple from what appeared to be a painful predicament.

The large jar of strawberry jam was wrestled down from Desiree's store cupboard and joined the bowl of cream on the table.

Tilly looked at the task before her, feeling more than a little daunted. She had big paws, which always seemed to get in the way of life's more delicate jobs, and had had quite a few run-ins with the office typewriter, which insisted on typing several letters at once. Neither had she ever been able to take just one sweet out of a bag when offered. More recently, there had been an issue with the telephone dial in the staff sideboard, where she regularly called wrong numbers, much to the annoyance of the cats on the other end of the line. Today, as she stared down at the batch of perfect scones, she very much doubted whether she could accurately split them with the knife that Desiree had put in front of her.

Apple instinctively moved over to help as she'd come to the end of her bap buttering. 'Shall I split while you cream and jam up?' she suggested, as Bonny coaxed the buttons on her concertina back into life and Desiree put the finishing touches to her savoury flans.

Tilly was pleased to escape the more specialised part of the job, but – faced with the first perfectly split scone – another problem loomed. 'Is it cream or jam first?' she shouted above the rather energetic set of Irish jigs spilling out of Bonny's concertina.

'Well, now – that *is* a question,' said Desiree. 'It depends on where you come from, and you've hit on one of the biggest disputes in the whole universe! Wars have been fought over jammin' and creamin'. In this household, we do it the Cornish way or Rooster gets upset – his lot hails from down there, so it's jam first then cream. But if you have the slightest touch of Devon about you, then it's cream first then jam. As you're doin' 'em, I think you should be allowed to choose. Whatever happens, they'll be lovely.'

Tilly was renowned for her even-pawed approach to problems and decided in an egalitarian fashion to do some of each. The first six scones went very well, using the jam-first method, and to celebrate, Desiree plated them up on one of her reusable lace doilies. The second six, using the Devonian method, went like a dream as Tilly plastered the cream on with a pallet knife – and then the trouble began. Apple's strawberry jam refused to stay put on top of the cream, no matter how aggressive Tilly became with the jam spoon. Dollops of jam slid off the scones and onto the table. Tilly's spoon was caked with cream, and, in the tussle for supremacy, Tilly became covered in it as well. To make matters worse, Blight Chit mistook the proceedings for a game of mud pies and launched himself into the bowl of clotted cream, covering Desiree and Apple with the splash he'd created. Bonny Grubb played on, and Desiree's boathouse became a sticky red and white disaster area; the concertina rose and fell as the avalanche of clotted cream and strawberry jam took over the table, the floor and the walls. Some of the scones clung to the roof as Blight tossed them into the air with such unbridled joy that it was impossible for his doting mother to be the slightest bit cross about the desecration of her home.

As with all storms, peace was eventually established when Desiree caught up with her overexcited kitten and deposited him out into the sunshine. Tilly and Apple salvaged as many scones as they could and resorted to a marble effect of jam and cream to top them, agreeing that the Neapolitan touch made them look extra special. Desiree prepared a bowl of hot, soapy water and had the surfaces and floor wiped clean in no time, and the four cats joined Blight out in the sunshine for a much-needed tea break while things dried off. Later that afternoon, no one would ever have believed that such chaos had existed in the creation of what all agreed was a magnificent spread.

CHAPTER TWENTY-ONE

Fluff Wither-Fork was still in shock when Hettie left her at the Hall to return to the allotments. She had reported her findings regarding Gertrude Jingle's past and her connection with the Wither-Spoons, but there had been a lot to take in and many unanswered questions remained, most of which needed to be discussed with Micks and Mash. There was still the matter of the murders, too, and Hettie had promised that the culprit would be found, no matter who he was; Miss Jingle's killing had been an act of extreme violence, and any cat capable of that needed to be stopped. Hettie's brief experience of murder had taught her that once a life had been taken, killing again was easy and often necessary to cover up what had gone before. There was now an urgency in solving the case before another body hit the ground, but, out of respect, the day belonged to Miss Jingle, and Hettie decided to suspend further enquiries until after the funeral.

Arrangements had certainly come on apace by the time she returned to the plot. The summer house had been reconstructed into a catafalque of sorts – an oblong box big enough to contain all Gertrude's worldly goods, including her ornate rocking chair. The site where the hut had stood was now a bare patch of earth. Morbid Balm was with Bruiser as Hettie approached. 'Anything I can do to help?' she asked, admiring the structure that now took centre stage. 'You've made a great job of this. It's high, isn't it?'

Morbid nodded. 'It had to be to fit all her stuff in. It's going to take quite an effort to get her up there, but it should look fantastic when we've decorated it with the lilies. We could do with stepladders at each corner, really, so we can lift her up in one go. Thinking about it, we could get the mattress up first as that's the heavy bit, then pop her on top afterwards.'

Bruiser nodded. 'That's a good plan. That way we won't run the risk of 'er rollin' off.'

'Shall I see if I can rustle up more stepladders from the other plots?' Hettie offered, distancing herself from any corpse-removing duties.

'Yeah, that'd be great,' said Morbid. 'We've got

just under an hour before midday, so we need to get a move on. I'll set the fire while you're doing that. I've brought some firelighters to dot round the base and the hut was nice and dry, so once we get it going the wood should take quite quickly. The secret is to get it all hot enough to burn the body, but I'm going to soak the mattress in barbecue fluid just to make sure.'

Hettie marvelled at the way in which Morbid handled her profession, going about her work in a matter-of-fact way without ever losing her reverence for the dead, and wanting every final journey to be executed to perfection under her care. Customer satisfaction was obviously key, in this world and the next. She bumped into Clippy Lean on the path as she went in search of more steps. The bus conductress had taken a rare day off, as she was keen to attend Miss Jingle's funeral. 'I wouldn't miss it for the world,' she said. 'I'll miss *her*, though. I used to have lovely chats with her when I brought her shopping in. I can't believe that anyone would want to hurt her. I just don't know what's happening around here any more, and to top it all someone has nicked off with my scarecrow.'

Under different circumstances, Hettie would have been interested in the disappearance of yet another scarecrow but, as Morbid had said, time was ticking on and she needed to complete her mission. 'I don't suppose you have such a thing as a pair of stepladders I can borrow?' she said hopefully.

'I haven't got any, but the Gamps have – two pairs, actually, but you'd expect that with them. Shall I go and ask for you? They've just arrived. I suppose they're coming to the funeral as well.'

Hettie could have hugged Clippy. She would never admit it, but she found the Gamp sisters a rather terrifying prospect at the best of times; to her, they came across as one of those monsters from ancient Greece with two heads on one body. 'That would be really kind of you,' Hettie said, following Clippy back down the path. 'I'll come and wait by the gate.'

The Gamp sisters proved to be a fruitful supply of stepladders, and Clippy soon reappeared with two identical sets. Hettie led the way back to Miss Jingle's plot, where the stepladders were gratefully received and immediately put to work. Rooster, Bruiser and Jeremiah were chosen as mattress-bearers, but they were still one short and all eyes turned to Tarragon Trench as the only other male available. One look confirmed that there was very little point in enlisting his help in anything practical, so Hettie stepped forward as the tallest of the female cats.

Morbid and Bruiser moved Miss Jingle's body off the mattress, laying it carefully down on the ground. The bearers carried the mattress across to where the four stepladders had been placed, one at each corner of the structure. Jeremiah and Rooster climbed their ladders, hauling the mattress up as they went, and

Hettie and Bruiser positioned themselves on top of the structure to receive it and put it in place. Morbid stood at the bottom, hoping that the extra weight wouldn't bring the whole thing down around their ears, but all was well and the team congratulated themselves on a job well done – even Jeremiah Corbit gave a grunt of satisfaction as he clambered back to earth. Hettie lingered for a moment on top of the mattress, her eye caught by a movement from the gatehouse turret; she expected it to be Micks, but surprisingly it was Mash who was staring out across at her.

'Right, just the body and the lilies,' shouted Morbid. Bruiser stepped forward, and Hettie suddenly felt obliged to help. Her conversation with Miss Jingle had been short, but it had left a lasting impression; the horror of the murder and the fact that the perpetrator had not yet been found made her want to perform a final act of respect by helping to place the body on the pyre. Under Morbid's instruction, Bruiser and Hettie carried Miss Jingle, using the knots at either end of the sheet that enclosed her. The burden was surprisingly light, and Gertrude was easily lifted up onto the mattress, ready for her cremation. Once again, Hettie glanced across at the gatehouse, but this time there was no sign of Micks or Mash.

The helpers melted away to their plots to change into their funeral clothes, leaving Morbid, Bruiser and Hettie to decorate the structure with Miss Jingle's lilies.

Morbid doused the mattress in barbecue fluid, then chose the biggest and most beautiful of the blooms to lay with the body, while Hettie and Bruiser tied more flowers to the sides of the pyre and scattered bulbs around the base.

Fluff Wither-Fork was the first of the mourners to arrive and she gasped at the spectacle before her. 'I've never seen anything so beautiful,' she said. 'Miss Balm, you have done us all a great service in turning such horror into something so magnificent. Miss Jingle would be delighted.'

Morbid beamed with pride at a job well done. Desiree Chit barged the gate open with a tray of ham baps, swiftly followed by Tilly and two plates piled high with cream and jam scones, none the worse for their earlier incident. Apple Chutney followed moments later with the savoury flans, and Fluff – needing to keep busy – helped to unload the food onto the trestle table, which she'd set up earlier. The funeral tea was coming along nicely as more plates arrived from the Chits' boathouse. Hettie was delighted to see a mountain of potato cakes, as well as some iced buns and a selection of puddings; the centrepiece was Desiree's special trifle, which she'd made in a washing-up bowl to ensure that there was enough to go round.

The funeral guests arrived one by one, all amazed at the sight before them. There was nothing macabre about the giant tower of lilies that guarded Miss Jingle's earthly remains; it was a truly magnificent sight, and those gathered together had to agree that it was a privilege to be part of it. Tilly had shaken off her oversized apron and stood next to Hettie and Bruiser, waiting for Morbid Balm to complete her task. Hettie stared round at the faces, looking for one that was etched with remorse or guilt: Clippy Lean, a pillar of the community, tidy and respectful; the Mulch sisters, dressed in matching flower-print frocks; Blackberry Tibbs in a clean white shirt; the Gamps in identical black; Corbit, who appeared to have combed his grizzly grey fur; the Chits, smart but casual; Apple Chutney, sporting a clean pair of dungarees and a little too much eye make-up; and Bonny Grubb, wearing an elaborate shawl to cover up her poor, well-mended clothes. None of them struck her as being capable of Miss Jingle's murder, but the Wither-Spoons were conspicuous by their absence. Grief-stricken? she wondered. Riddled with guilt? Or simply watching from their ivory tower?

'Ivory tower!' exclaimed Hettie suddenly, and all eyes turned to her. 'That's it!'

The sun was almost at its highest point in the sky. Undeterred by Hettie's outburst, Morbid stepped forward. She climbed one of the stepladders and opened the small funeral pot, sprinkling its contents over the body and leaving the empty pot to burn. She removed the steps to a safe distance and proceeded to light the base of the pyre with her matches. The wood took immediately, and within seconds flames were leaping up into the cloudless sky. Morbid stood back from the heat, praying that there would be no wind to divert the course of the fire as it began to consume Miss Jingle's life, and eventually her body.

The heat drove the onlookers away from the inferno, and the funeral tea became the main attraction. The cats gathered round the trestle table, occasionally looking back at the progress of the cremation. Miss Jingle's mattress burnt quickly, allowing the body to slip down into the heart of the fire where it was quickly consumed. It would be several hours before the ashes could be raked into the soil, and days before the smoke would die down, but if there was to be a reincarnation of Miss Jingle, all had been done to assist it.

CHAPTER TWENTY-TWO

The funeral party broke up once the trestle tables had been picked clean, and everyone returned to their allotments to chew over the day's extraordinary event. Fluff Wither-Fork had been the first to leave, having no appetite for food or socialising. Hettie, Tilly, Bruiser and Morbid were the only cats left on-site as the sun began to sink in the west, signalling the end of the cremation. Morbid had been the star of the day. Her attention to detail was widely admired, and she had actually picked up some advance business for Shroud and Trestle over the scones and ham baps. Hettie's head was now full of possibilities regarding the murders, and although she was keen to pay a call on Micks and Mash, she decided to put it off until the morning. She needed time to consider and process all the information surrounding the case, and knew that a peaceful evening with a pipe or two of catnip was the way to go.

When Morbid was satisfied that the smoking remains of the cremation were safe, the four cats closed the gate on what had been Miss Jingle's allotment and made their way back to the main road, where Miss Scarlet was parked. Morbid gratefully accepted a lift back to the undertakers, where she had left her bicycle, and clambered onto the back of the motorbike behind Bruiser. Hettie and Tilly took their place in the sidecar.

The gatehouse was in darkness, which Hettie thought was a little strange as the parkland was floodlit with cats coming and going like tiny ants in the distance. The Michaelmas Flower and Produce Show was clearly coming together, with or without the Wither-Spoons. Tomorrow would be the harvest festival – the anniversary of Lettuce Wither-Fork's accident, and the day when all the Wither-Fork residents would offer up their vegetables, flowers and thankful prayers in the small church, presided over by the Reverend Augusta Stitch. And it was her bread van that nearly drove Miss Scarlet off the road at the foot of Wither-Fork Hill. 'Bloody idiot!' said Hettie as Bruiser swerved, mounted the grass verge, removing a small section of the hedgerow, and returned them to the road unscathed. 'What the hell is she doing driving about in an old bread van? Why can't she have a Morris Minor like the Reverend Mulch had?'

Tilly giggled, recovering from the jolt. 'I suppose she thinks she's delivering the bread of heaven to her flock,' she quipped.

Hettie couldn't resist joining in. 'Yes, and it puts a new spin on five loaves and two bloody fishes! Although I doubt she could perform a miracle if it bit her on the . . .'

A bump in the road saved Miss Scarlet's sidecar from the expletives, and Bruiser brought her to a standstill outside Shroud and Trestle, where Morbid – reunited with her bicycle – headed for home. Hettie made an on-the-spot decision to stop once more before the three friends made tracks for their own cosy firesides, and Bruiser responded by applying the brakes outside Elsie Haddock's fish emporium. Hettie leapt out of the sidecar and returned minutes later with three hot parcels of fish and chips, and Bruiser gave Miss Scarlet full throttle as the cats sped down the high street, salivating over the prospect of a hot supper. He dropped Hettie and Tilly at the front of the Butters' pie and pastry shop, and drove off to enjoy his supper in his shed at the bottom of the garden, where Miss Scarlet also had her own shelter. Hettie and Tilly made their way down the passageway that led to the backyard and the official entrance to their room at the back of the bakery. Tilly set to with the fire while Hettie filled the kettle, and both cats were about to abandon their day clothes when there was a knock at the door. The dulcet tones of Betty Butter rang out. 'Got a visitor for you. She's been waiting upstairs with us.'

Hettie flung open the door in a somewhat irritated fashion. She'd seen enough cats for one day, and the last thing she needed was an unexpected visitor encroaching on what she liked to call her 'downtime'. Betty beat a hasty retreat back up to her flat, leaving Hettie's visitor to introduce herself. 'I am so terribly sorry to bother you,' she said, 'but I was told that you might be able to help me. My name is Binky Crustworthy, and I'm looking for my brother, Bartlet.'

Hettie stared at the cat for a moment, taking in her rather strange outfit. She was dressed from head to toe in country tweeds, with a matching cape and a deerstalker hat, which she held in her paws rather nervously, twisting it as she spoke. The brindle-coloured cat gave off an overpowering smell of mothballs, as if she spent her days in an old wardrobe. 'Please come in,' she said, as Tilly scrabbled round trying to make their cosy bedsitter look like an office. 'Would you like a cup of tea?'

Binky shook her head. 'That's very kind of you, but your landladies have just treated me to sandwiches and cake. I'm absolutely fine for the moment.'

Hettie offered the cat a seat at the table, which now looked more like a desk. Tilly had whipped the rather stained gingham tablecloth off and replaced it with

Hettie's diary, which she never used, and a selection of pens and pencils. There was nothing to be done about the smell of fish and chips that filled the room, now punctuated by mothballs, but Tilly reasoned with herself that it *was* dinner time. 'Now,' said Hettie. 'You say you're looking for your brother, Bartlet?'

'Yes, that's right. He had some business at Wither-Fork Hall on Monday and I haven't heard from him since.'

Hettie shared a look with Tilly, knowing that they were about to solve the identity of the dead stranger on Bonny Grubb's onion patch, but she let Binky Crustworthy continue, 'My brother and I run a charity called the National Crust. We save historic buildings and invest our money in preservation. A lot of our work involves setting up housing in these buildings for cats who find themselves homeless through no fault of their own. Bartlet is rather good at cat-lets, as we like to call them – self-contained "des res" with communal responsibilities. "Reserve to preserve" is our motto. No building too big, no venture too small. Anyway, where was I? Oh yes – we received a letter from Miss Wither-Fork, asking if we might be interested in taking on her property and land as she was having difficulty in propping the place up. My brother, Bartlet, was very excited at the prospect, as Wither-Fork Hall is a fine specimen of Jacobean architecture, unsullied by modernisers. He made an appointment to look round the property and see if we might take it on. He suggested last Monday, and – as he heard nothing to the contrary – set out for Wither-Fork on his motorbike. That's the last I saw of him. He's never away from Crustworthy Manor for more than a night or two, and he always phones to let me know when he's due back. I'm now very worried, and the cat I spoke to this afternoon at the Wither-Fork gatehouse said she hadn't seen him. I returned to the town and went to the post office in case he'd been in to send me a telegram or something, and the postmistress said you were detectives and might be able to help. I fear that he may have had an accident en route, and could be lying in a hospital bed or a ditch. He's a bit of a maverick when he hits the open road on his beloved motorbike. It wouldn't be the first time he's come off the thing.'

Hettie hated to be the bearer of bad news, but the help that she and Tilly could offer amounted to a trip to Shroud and Trestle, where Bartlet Crustworthy was currently a non-paying guest. To avoid any unnecessary grief, Hettie had to make sure. She nodded to Tilly, who brought the sketchbook over to the table. Binky Crustworthy pounced on it. 'Where did you find this?' she asked, looking relieved until she caught the look on Hettie's face.

'I'm so very sorry to tell you that I believe your brother was killed on Wither-Fork allotments some time on Monday night or early Tuesday morning.'

216

Binky stared at Hettie in disbelief. 'I don't believe you,' she said. 'How can he be dead? And what do you mean, "killed"? How can you be killed on an allotment? That's ridiculous. It can't be him. I'd know if he were dead. You must have made a mistake.' Binky Crustworthy stared down at the sketchbook in her paws, absent-mindedly flicking through the pages as her tears added to the watercolours that had been so skilfully painted by her brother. 'Please tell me – how did the accident happen?' she asked, not really wanting to know.

Hettie felt that at this stage there was no point in softening the blow. 'I'm afraid your brother was murdered. We're investigating his death and another killing up on the allotments.'

'Murdered!' cried Binky. 'Who would want to murder Bartlet? This is a nightmare. And another killing, you say? Where is my brother now? The cat at the gatehouse said there was a funeral this afternoon – surely he hasn't been buried without me?' Binky Crustworthy began to rock with grief, her sobs coming loud and fast. All Hettie and Tilly could do was wait until things became a little calmer before explaining the whereabouts of Bartlet Crustworthy.

Tilly boiled the kettle and made three mugs of sweet, milky tea. Hettie offered the fire another shovel of coal and returned to the table, where Binky's sobs had become more of a whimper, interrupted by the occasional gulp. Her face, paws and tweed suit were

217

soaked in tears, and Tilly proffered a tea towel to help with the worst of it. Binky blew her nose and wiped her eyes, gratefully accepting the mug of tea, which she clutched to her for warmth and comfort. 'Is there anyone we can contact for you?' asked Tilly.

Binky shook her head. 'No, there's no one – not now, anyway. It was always me and Bartlet. Please tell me where he is. It wasn't *his* funeral, was it?'

'No,' said Hettie. 'He's being looked after by our local undertaker. Would you like me to call them for you?'

'That would be most kind. I can't even remember where my car is. I think I may have parked it outside the post office.'

Hettie and Tilly shared a look. If Lavender Stamp had anything to do with it, the car would have been towed away by now; she took great exception to any cat parking outside her post office, except for the library van, which brought in more customers. Tilly crawled into the staff sideboard and pulled the telephone out. Hettie dialled and got Mr Shroud himself, who was very pleased to be able to put a name to the stranger in one of his refrigeration drawers. He counselled that if a viewing was to take place, Morbid would need to 'tidy things up', and that would take an hour or so as she had gone home for the day. Hettie rang off, having made the appointment for Binky, who sat hunched at the table.

'I'll go and see if I can find your car,' said Tilly, needing to do something helpful. 'What does it look like?'

'It's blue with mud all over it. Bartlet was going to wash it for me, but . . .' Binky Crustworthy collapsed again in a sobbing heap, and Tilly flew out of the door, leaving Hettie to staunch the flow with another tea towel. The car was indeed outside the post office, covered in mud with one of Lavender Stamp's abusive little notes stuck to the windscreen. There were no official parking restrictions, but Lavender was a law unto herself, and the very thought of any cat clogging up what she regarded as her shop frontage threw her into a rage, tempered only by the hit-and-run delivery of one of her nasty bits of paper.

An hour, two very damp tea towels and three mugs of tea later, Hettie and Tilly waved Binky Crustworthy off as she set out for Shroud and Trestle to claim the body of her brother Bartlet. Hettie had offered to accompany her for support, but was pleased and relieved when the offer was declined. Binky had decided to make the necessary arrangements to have Bartlet's body delivered to Crustworthy Manor, where he was to be buried in the family vault. She asked that Hettie keep her up to date with the murder enquiry, but refused the offer of a night on Betty and Beryl Butters' sofa, choosing instead to return home after identifying the body.

CHAPTER TWENTY-THREE

Hettie's mind was racing when they returned to their room. It had been frustrating to offer a sympathetic ear to Binky Crustworthy while so many revelations were swimming round in her head. She knew that the case was close to being cracked, but her thoughts needed to be ordered, and the only way to do that was to sit down with Tilly and sift through what they knew in the hope that all would become clear.

No sooner had they closed the door than their peace was shattered again, but this time in the best of ways. Seeing the look on Hettie's face, Tilly opened the door and was pleased to see Beryl Butter. 'Sister said you'd brought these in for your supper. Stone cold, they were, so we collected them while you were waving your visitor off and showed them the oven for a few minutes. Nice and hot now, and Betty's added a couple of iced cream slices for your pudding.'

Tilly accepted the hot parcels of fish and chips, and Hettie took charge of the cakes, using up her last beaming smile of the day on their landlady. They wasted no time in devouring their supper. Tilly – almost too full to move – tidied the fish and chip papers away into the coal scuttle for burning. Hettie threw off her clothes and replaced them with her dressing gown, then reached for her pipe and catnip pouch.

'So where do we go from here?' Tilly asked, struggling with the buttons on her pyjama top. 'We know the dead stranger is Bartlet Crustworthy, but why doesn't Miss Wither-Fork know who he was if he came to see her?'

'Well, that's the whole point,' said Hettie, blowing her first smoke ring into the fire. 'I suspect that Fluff Wither-Fork had no idea that Bartlet Crustworthy was coming to see her because she never got the reply to her letter. She told us that no one was interested in taking on her property.'

'So do you think it got lost in the post?'

'No, I think it got lost at the gatehouse. We know that Mash Wither-Spoon takes the mail to the Hall for her sister, so she could easily have kept Bartlet's reply to herself.'

'Why would she do that? She knows the money's running out and that Fluff's in dire straits – or at least she was before Miss Jingle's legacy.'

'I think Micks and Mash have every reason to fear anyone who attempts to take on Wither-Fork Hall. Fluff is a soft touch as far as her sister's concerned, and the Wither-Spoons suffer none of the day-to-day hardships that she has. Just think – if the National Crust *had* taken on the property, the chances are that Micks and Mash would be trading in their glorious little castle for one of Bartlet Crustworthy's cat-lets at the Hall. The gatehouse would be perfect for a visitor centre and a shop selling jams and tea towels.'

'I suppose that goes for all of the allotment holders,' Tilly pointed out. 'Perhaps Bartlet would have rehoused them as well. I can't see Bonny Grubb living in a cat-let and giving up her caravan, and Jeremiah Corbit's compost heaps wouldn't look great on the lawn in front of the Hall. Gertrude Jingle would never have left her lilies, either. It might turn out to be like one of Agatha Crispy's stories, where they all got together and murdered him, and then Miss Jingle threatened to tell and had to be silenced.'

Hettie had to concede that it wouldn't be the first time Agatha Crispy's work had inspired them in solving a case, but this time things were a little more complicated. 'Let's forget about Bartlet Crustworthy's murder for a minute and look at the death of Miss Jingle,' she said, reloading her pipe. 'I agree with you – I think she was killed because she knew something, but I'm not sure it was entirely connected with the first murder, although I do think the killings are linked. I can't remember her exact words when I spoke to her, but she said that Micks Wither-Spoon lived in an ivory tower. Well, that suggests to me that he's not responsible for anything he does, especially as Mash seems to spend her life protecting him.'

Tilly leapt up and dragged her dictionary out of the staff sideboard. 'Let me see,' she said, pawing through the tome that was almost as big as she was. 'Ah, here it is. "Ivory tower. Secluded place of shelter. State of being far removed from the harsh realities of life. An unworldly dreamer."'

'Exactly!' said Hettie. '"Shelter" is the big word there, and "removed from the harsh realities of life". That's what Mash does for him, but the big question is how far would she go to protect him, and what is he capable of in the strange world that he inhabits? The one consistent thing that everyone we've spoken to agrees on is that Micks Wither-Spoon lives in a world of his own. And what about Miss Jingle's letter to Fluff Wither-Fork? She suggests that Mash will need propping up at some point in the future, and that Micks is a danger to himself. That's a warning of bad stuff to come, if ever there was one. And

Binky Crustworthy said that Bartlet got here on his motorbike. Could that have been the same one that Micks drove away on yesterday?'

Tilly was excited now. Putting all the evidence together was one of her favourite parts of the cases they'd worked on, and she had a few observations of her own to add. 'It's odd that Mash wasn't more helpful to Binky Crustworthy when she called at the gatehouse today. Mash told her that she hadn't seen Bartlet, even though she knew that there'd been a body on Bonny's onion patch. Surely she should have put two and two together? And if the motorbike *was* Bartlet's, perhaps she thought they should get rid of it after Binky had been. And why is Micks in such a state that they can't now give their *Macbeth* at the show? He looked suicidal, perched on his battlements this morning, and they didn't come to Miss Jingle's cremation, which is really strange as they got on so well with her. Even if Micks didn't know they were related, you'd think they'd have turned up out of respect.'

Hettie put her pipe down in the hearth and absent-mindedly reached for a cream slice, pleased with their deductions so far. Tilly did the same, and for a few minutes there was much lip-smacking; her teeth were past their best, and sucking the cream out of any cake had become a ritual she enjoyed, especially if it had been baked by one of the Butter sisters.

The clock on the staff sideboard told them it was nearly midnight, and it had been a very long day. Hettie yawned. 'I think we'll interview Micks Wither-Spoon tomorrow, regardless of Mash's protestations. It's long overdue. Ivory tower or not, I intend to break the walls down and get to the bottom of this case come hell or high water.'

'I want to know where the scarecrows are disappearing to,' said Tilly, settling down on her blanket.

'I think that's for another day,' Hettie replied before falling into a deep sleep.

CHAPTER TWENTY-FOUR

The morning ritual of hot sweet tea and cheese triangles on toast was sidelined by Hettie's need to pay a month's rent to the Butters before Fluff Wither-Fork's fee burnt a hole in the pocket of her business slacks. Unusually bright, she dressed and left Tilly choosing clothes from the filing cabinet, returning with three sausage baps and three extra-milky frothy coffees – or lappes, as Tilly liked to call them. 'The rent's paid up and Bruiser's on his way up to join us for breakfast,' she said. 'I thought I'd treat us to something substantial. I think it's going to be another difficult day. I've ordered pies for supper and cream horns for afters. Betty said she'd leave them by the bread ovens if we were late back.'

Tilly clapped her paws at the thought of a cream horn and was energised by Hettie's mood. It was rare to see Hettie Bagshot bright-eyed and bushy-tailed before ten o'clock in the morning, and she admired the sense of purpose that her friend had adopted. 'Do you think today's the day?' she asked.

'I do,' said Hettie, taking a large bite of her bap. 'Case solved by teatime or I'm a short-haired black cat.'

Bruiser was less cheerful when he arrived at their door, having sat up late into the night with his new edition of *Biker's Monthly*. The sausage bap cheered him up immediately, and Hettie sketched out her plan of campaign for the day. 'It's Micks and Mash first, even if we have to break their door down,' she said, wiping the frothy bit of the coffee from her whiskers. 'Bruiser, I've got a special job for you while Tilly and I are with the Wither-Spoons. I want you to check and see if there's a motorbike anywhere near the gatehouse. If you can't find one, go for a run on Miss Scarlet and have a scout round. It's mostly countryside beyond Wither-Fork, so a quick look in fields and ditches would be good. If Micks Wither-Spoon has tried to get rid of it, it won't be far away.'

'What sort of bike is it?' asked Bruiser, always keen to discuss the finer points of his passion.

Hettie thought for a moment and realised that she had no idea. 'Two wheels, and it made a lot of noise,' she said lamely.

Bruiser grinned, showing all the teeth he didn't have. 'Right-o. Leave that one with me.'

Tilly made an ineffectual attempt at tidying their room before they emerged into the sunshine, ready to do battle at Wither-Fork Hall. Miss Scarlet was ready and waiting and parked outside the post office, much to Hettie's amusement. Lavender Stamp was lurking by her postbox, ready to pounce as Bruiser kicked the engine into life. Hettie and Tilly clambered aboard the sidecar and pulled their lid shut just as she reached them, and Miss Scarlet sped away leaving the postmistress in a cloud of white smoke.

Miss Scarlet climbed Wither-Fork Hill with ease, passing Clippy Lean's bus, which was stationary halfway up. Clearly today was not a good one for the ageing bus, but Hettie noticed that the stranded passengers were far from annoyed as they sat playing board games while waiting for the mechanic. There was no sign of Clippy, but Hettie – if she'd been a gambling cat – would have put money on the bus conductress being busy lifting potatoes on her allotment for the Michaelmas Show. Bruiser parked the bike and sidecar outside the gatehouse. There was no sign of Micks on his battlements; in fact, the gatehouse looked gloomy and unoccupied as Hettie and Tilly made their way round to the back door. The kitchen curtains were drawn closed, and there was no sign of life.

Hettie knocked on the door and waited. There was no reply so she knocked again, this time with more urgency. Still there was nothing, so she put her ear to the door to see if she could detect any sound from inside. All was silent.

'Don't you two ever give up?'

The voice came from behind them, and Mash Wither-Spoon appeared from the direction of the Hall. Hettie turned and was instantly shocked by her thin, drawn appearance; her eyes were puffy, and she looked like she'd slept in her clothes for several days. Gone was the buoyant, personable cat, and in her place stood a shambling wreck, hardly strong enough to put one paw in front of another. Hettie had planned a showdown with the Wither-Spoons, but now she could see that Mash was in no fit state for a heavy-paw approach. 'There are a few questions we need to ask you,' she said politely. 'Would this be a good time?'

Mash allowed a weak smile to cross her face. 'There aren't going to be any more good times, but you can come in and ask your questions if you like.' She felt in her pocket for the key and opened the back door. Hettie and Tilly followed her into the kitchen and sat down on the chairs offered to them. 'I'm having a cup of tea. Would you like one? I'm afraid there's no milk. I've run out.'

Hettie and Tilly refused the drink and watched

as Mash moved around the kitchen. The kettle had hardly boiled before she poured the water into a mug and added what appeared to be a herbal tea from a jam jar by the sink. The room was cold, dark and unwelcoming. The kitchen range was out and there were unwashed pots in the sink and several opened tins abandoned on the table, half-eaten with spoons sticking out of them. It was a far cry from the chaos of the *Macbeth* rehearsals that Hettie and Tilly had witnessed earlier in the week; that had at least been happy chaos, but now it was obvious that there was something very wrong with Mash Wither-Spoon and her kitchen.

Mash brought her drink to the table and slumped down on a chair, sipping from the mug in a distracted way, as if there was no one else in the room with her. Hettie gave a polite cough to attract her attention, but Mash continued to stare down at her drink until she'd drained the mug and pushed it away from her. 'So fire away,' she said unexpectedly, catching Hettie out. 'Let's get your questions answered, and then you can leave me in peace.'

Hettie responded as Tilly pulled out her notebook. 'I'd like to talk to you about a cat called Bartlet Crustworthy. I believe you may have met him recently?'

'Ah yes. Charming manners and high hopes of taking on Wither-Fork Hall, lock, stock and barrel. He thought he was talking to Fluff when he turned up here on Monday, and I didn't disillusion him. He had such great plans for the estate. Turning the Hall into flats, opening a garden centre on the allotments, motorbike and vintage car rallies on the parkland – and he wanted to turn the gatehouse into a museum dedicated to Lettuce Wither-Fork, complete with gift shop.'

Hettie was taken aback at Mash's carefree admission, but stuck to her questions. 'Did your sister know he was coming?'

'Of course not. I intercepted his letter before it got to her. She's been wanting to give the place away for years, with no thought of what might happen to me and Micks. Crustworthy just turned up here on Monday and started throwing his plans about as if he owned the place already.'

'So what happened after he'd discussed his plans with you?'

Mash smiled again. 'You know what happened,' she said. 'I took him up to the allotments after dark and bashed his brains out with a rock.'

'*You* did!' said Hettie. 'Are you sure it wasn't Micks who killed him?'

'Perfectly sure. Micks stayed here practising his lines.'

'And did you tell Micks what you'd done?'

'In a roundabout way. I told him that Bartlet Crustworthy wouldn't be bothering us again. Micks was perfectly happy with that.' Mash rose from the table and made another drink for herself, this time not offering one to Hettie or Tilly.

Tilly scribbled as quietly as she could in her notebook, and Hettie decided to raise the subject of Gertrude Jingle.

When Mash returned to her seat, she wasted no time with a preamble. 'Did you kill Gertrude Jingle as well?'

Mash smiled again. 'Well, that's a little more complicated and there may not be time to give you the full picture.'

'Why's that?' asked Hettie, looking puzzled.

'Because the process has begun and there is very little time left,' Mash replied, draining her drink once more.

With horror, Hettie realised what was happening. 'What are you drinking?' she demanded. 'That's not tea, is it?'

'Essence of lily flower. Very poisonous to cats. A parting gift from dear Miss Jingle.'

Hettie suddenly remembered the bunch of lilies that had been abandoned on the draining board the last time they were in the Wither-Spoons' kitchen. 'Why are you doing this? We need to get you some help. You should make yourself sick!' Hettie and Tilly were thrown into a panic, but Mash sat calmly on her chair, completely resigned to her fate. Once more, Hettie tried to head off the inevitable. 'What about Micks? He can't live without you. Think what you're doing before it's too late.'

'It *is* too late, and I thought you wanted to know about Miss Jingle?'

'I do,' said Hettie, very disturbed by what was happening in front of her.

'Then let's see how far we get. After I'd killed Bartlet Crustworthy, Miss Jingle sent for me on Tuesday afternoon. She was very agitated and seemed to think that Micks was involved in Crustworthy's death. She told me that she had a confession to make and took me into her summer house, where we could talk privately. The story she told me was quite bizarre. She said she'd run away with a maharaja and made a life for herself in India, but before she went she'd had a boy kitten that her sister, Scoop, and Lorrie Wither-Spoon had adopted. She said she couldn't have kept the kitten because the maharaja wouldn't have wanted her if he'd known. The kitten was Micks, and the Wither-Spoons travelled from theatre to theatre, dragging Micks around with them. Gertrude told me that his adoptive father beat him and treated him very badly. Her sister did nothing to protect him, and as soon as Micks was old enough he fought back. She also told me that she was convinced that Micks had stabbed the Wither-Spoons to death in their dressing room, locked the door and waited for the theatre staff to break it down after he'd spent two days with their bodies. No one suspected him, and he was put in an orphanage until he was old enough to leave. That's when I met Micks and we fell for each other in a big way. He was fragile and haunted by what had happened to him, and I came along at the right moment. I believed in his version of the story. Even when one of the other cats on our method-acting course was stabbed to death I didn't connect it with Micks in any way. Thinking about it now, he was very keen to leave the course and come and set up home here at Wither-Fork. We were happy until Gertrude arrived on the allotments and started taking an interest in him. Now I know why.'

All suddenly became clear to Hettie. 'You're about to tell me that Micks murdered Miss Jingle?' The 'yes' was whispered and Mash bowed her head, allowing her tears to splash onto the kitchen table. Hettie could see that time was running out. Justice was slowly being served in front of her, but there were still questions. 'What made Micks kill Miss Jingle? It was you she told, not Micks.'

Mash lifted her head with a great effort. 'I came home and told him that Gertrude was his mother. I challenged him about what Gertrude had told me, expecting him to say that it wasn't true, but he just cried with rage. I've never seen him like that. He said she'd destroyed his life by walking out on him and leaving him with the Wither-Spoons. I tried to stop him, but he just flew out of the door. He came back an hour later, covered in blood with a large bunch of lilies, and just sat by the stove in his chair, reciting his lines and staring at his bloody paws. "This is a sorry sight." He kept saying that over and over again. Eventually, he slept, and the next morning he was his old self. I washed his bloody clothes and we set the kitchen up to rehearse, and that's when you came to see us. I wasn't really sure what he'd done until Blackberry Tibbs came to fetch you. Then I knew the game was up, which was why I couldn't let you question him. He'd have probably told you everything, and I had to protect him while I thought what to do.'

'And what did you do?' asked Hettie gently.

Mash stood up, but was very unsteady. Tilly moved to help her, but she refused assistance. 'Come with me. You may as well see the end of our little play.' She moved towards the stairs, grabbing the rail for support and using all her strength to haul herself up the steps one by one. Hettie and Tilly followed at a discreet distance.

The stairs opened out into the turret room they'd heard so much about. It was medieval in design, with tapestry hangings on the walls, a large four-poster bed, and arched windows overlooking the parkland of Wither-Fork Hall. On the other side of the room was a further short flight of steps with a door that led out onto the roof, giving Micks his favourite vantage point. The door was closed. There was no sign of Micks.

Mash faltered and fell to the floor. Hettie and Tilly both moved to help her and half-dragged, half-carried her to the four-poster. Tilly pulled the curtains back and suddenly realised that the bed was occupied. There, laid out in death, was Micks Wither-Spoon. With the very last of her strength, Mash crawled onto the bed beside him, holding him close to her. Her final words were slurred, but they could just be made out. '"A glooming peace this morning with it brings; The sun, for sorrow, will not show his head: Go hence, to have more talk of these sad things: Some shall be pardon'd, and some punished: For never was a story of more woe Than this of Juliet and her Romeo."'

Hettie and Tilly stood silently as the final breath left Mash Wither-Spoon's body. The scene was a beautiful one, and regardless of the horror that had brought them all to this moment, Hettie would have wanted it no other way. Micks and Mash were soulmates in life and now in death. As often happens, one small mistake had created a life of tragedy. In the peace of the turret room, Hettie considered the victims: Bartlet Crustworthy, perhaps a little too enthusiastic about changing cats' lives; Gertrude Jingle, living a lie that eventually consumed her; Micks Wither-Spoon, locked in his ivory tower where nothing could hurt any more; and Mash, the real victim – like Juliet, the only one who had died for love.

A pounding on the gatehouse door broke the silence, sending a jolt through Hettie and Tilly that was both painful and disturbing. Hettie drew the bed curtains closed on Micks' and Mash's final scene, and left the turret room with Tilly as the hammering continued. Fluff Wither-Fork pushed past them as Hettie opened the door. 'Where is she?' she panted, out of breath. 'I must speak to her before she does anything stupid.'

Tilly barred the way to the turret-room stairs as Hettie held Fluff back. 'I'm afraid there's nothing you can do,' she said. 'It's over, and under the circumstances it's probably all for the best.' Hettie's words sounded hollow and unfeeling, especially to her, but there was no time to think of anything clever or sympathetic. There were no appropriate stock phrases to deal with what lay upstairs in the four-poster bed, and Mash Wither-Spoon's final exit speech would take a lot of beating, even though she had borrowed it.

Fluff slumped down on the kitchen chair that had so recently been vacated by her sister, and Hettie and Tilly joined her at the table. She stared at the empty mug in front of her, turning it in her paws before finding some words to express her sorrow. 'Mash came to me this morning and told me she'd killed a cat from the National Crust. She said that Micks had murdered Miss Jingle because she was his mother, and that late last night she'd poisoned Micks. I laughed at her. I thought she was trying out one of her stupid plays on me. She got angry and accused me of destroying her life. She said that I'd never accepted Micks and that I was scheming to take their home away from them. She got up and left before I had a chance to say anything, but on her way out she said that the gatehouse would be vacant by the end of the day. I let her go. I just thought she was having one of her tantrums, and then the phone rang and it was the wretched Augusta Stitch going on about the harvest festival. After she rang off, I tried to come to terms with what Mash had told me, but how could I honestly believe that she'd killed anyone, let alone Micks? He was the centre of her life, the reason she got up in the morning, and then it hit me – she couldn't possibly live without him. I ran all the way from the Hall, because suddenly I knew what she was going to do. Where is she now?'

'She's with Micks,' said Hettie. 'She'd planned it all down to the very last detail, and if it's any consolation her death was painless and peaceful. They're together upstairs in the turret room.'

Fluff was silent for some time, then gathered herself and climbed the stairs, leaving Hettie and Tilly in the kitchen. They sat silently, waiting for her return. When she reappeared in the kitchen, the old air of authority had returned to her and she addressed Hettie directly. 'Miss Bagshot, I would appreciate your discretion in this matter for a couple of days. It will all come out in the end, but I would like some time to grieve before my sister's death is hijacked by the media. To avoid bringing attention to this tragedy, I intend to let the harvest festival and the Michaelmas Show go ahead.

So many cats have put their time into the events, and I must bear the burden of my family's shame, not my tenants or workers. I am in your debt for handling this whole situation in such a diplomatic and professional way, and I will make sure that your account is settled accordingly. I'm going to lock up the gatehouse and leave things as they are until the show is over. I'll have to make arrangements for the Wither-Fork tomb to be opened, but I daresay Morbid Balm will be able to assist with the practicalities.'

Hettie nodded in agreement, and she and Tilly followed Fluff to the door, leaving the gatehouse with its sad secret to brood while the rest of the estate and its visitors looked forward to two days of celebration.

CHAPTER TWENTY-FIVE

Without any further conversation, Fluff Wither-Fork left Hettie and Tilly at the gatehouse and made her way back to the Hall. With the case solved and the perpetrators quite literally laid to rest, the No. 2 Feline Detective Agency had time on its paws. There were a few loose ends to clear up, though, and one of those bedraggled threads had just come to a noisy standstill at the gates of Wither-Fork Hall. Bruiser leapt off the motorbike that Micks Wither-Spoon had driven away so recently and grinned at them. 'Found it a couple of miles down the road behind a haystack,' he said, removing his helmet. 'Keys were still in the ignition. I'm surprised no one had nicked it. Nice bike; runnin' a bit rough, but nothing a good tune-up wouldn't fix. I've left Miss Scarlet where I found this, so I'll 'ave to walk back and pick 'er up – unless you fancy tryin' yer skills out?'

Bruiser addressed the invitation directly to Hettie, who shrank back as if he'd burnt her with a poker. When they bought Miss Scarlet from Lazarus Hambone's yard in the town, it was hoped that Hettie would be proficient enough to master the road after a few lessons. The fact of the matter was that she much preferred to travel in style with Tilly in the sidecar, and since Bruiser had turned up, she'd shown no interest whatsoever in becoming a biker cat. She looked up at the blue September sky and then back to Bruiser. 'It's such a lovely day for a walk. Why don't you go and fetch Miss Scarlet, and Tilly and I will check out the vendors at the Hall for lunch? We could meet you near the church in about an hour.'

Bruiser grinned again and put the keys to Bartlet Crustworthy's motorbike in her paw. 'Right-o. I'll wheel this into the yard and be off.' He left the motorbike in the backyard of the gatehouse and set off into the countryside at a brisk pace. Hettie and Tilly waved him off and made their way through the gates to the Hall, crossing the parkland to where the tents and marquee stood ready for the Michaelmas Show. There had been much activity inside the main marquee, with trestle tables covered in green tablecloths set up round the edge and labelled in sections for judging: potatoes; marrows; cabbages; peas and beans; carrots; onions and leeks; courgettes; beetroot; cucumbers; tomatoes; and radishes. There was a large set of weighing scales by the table to record the magnitude of the crops, and a box of red, blue and yellow rosettes waiting to be awarded to the lucky winners.

'I really don't see the point of vegetables,' said Hettie. 'Not when there's meat and pastry to eat. Cats who eat vegetables are thin and sly in my experience.'

'That's because they're waiting to pounce on a pie when no one's looking,' said Tilly. 'But some vegetables are nice. The Butters' meat and potato pie would be a bit sad without potatoes, and what would we do without Elsie Haddock's chips or all those crisps we like?'

Hettie had to concede that Tilly had a point and immediately cheered up as a rather officious-looking cat started labelling the tables on the other side of the marquee. The subject matter here was much more to Hettie's taste, with pies of every possible combination: pork; steak and kidney; sausage; veal and ham; minced beef; chicken; and cheese. The labels heralded the coming of so many delights that she began to feel quite faint with hunger, and was about to suggest an appetiser before lunch from one of the outside stalls when the cat giving out the labels approached.

'I'm sorry but you can't be in here,' he said, much to

Hettie's amusement as she clearly *was* 'in here'. 'You know the rules,' the cat continued. 'If you're exhibiting, there's no entry until the labels are out and you've collected your exhibitor's number at the gate and the corresponding tag to place on your entries – unless they're in the pastry class, in which case they should be freshly baked and placed in position tomorrow morning. No pastry on site until the day of the judging. Have I made myself clear?' Tilly stifled a snigger as Hettie nodded sagely, inciting the cat to continue with his rules and regulations. 'We don't spend our time drawing up a comprehensive pack of exhibitors' notes for you to just ignore them, you know. Don't think for a minute that my time stops when the show finishes. The plans for next year's show are well underway and there are going to be changes, you mark my words. It won't be so easy to get a place in here next year, so you'd better make the most of it because you might not be eligible in future. I think I should warn you that this breach in regulations hasn't gone unnoticed, and, as top and supreme judge, I am within my rights to bar you from the marquee altogether for this year and most probably in perpetuity.'

The tirade was clearly set to continue, but it stopped dead at the sound of Fluff Wither-Fork's voice as she entered the marquee. 'Ah, Mr Stickler. I see you've met Miss Bagshot and Miss Jenkins. They are my guests here at Wither-Fork and have the run of the place, so please offer them every courtesy as I'm hoping to persuade them to help with the presentations this year.'

Hettie and Tilly beamed at Fluff Wither-Fork, and Mr Stickler dismounted from his high horse and began bowing and scraping in a very unpleasant manner. 'Of course, Miss Wither-Fork. I was just telling our young friends here all about the—'

Fluff held her paw up to Stickler's face, bringing the conversation to an end before turning to Hettie. 'I'd be very pleased if you and Miss Jenkins would join me for a late informal supper after the harvest festival this evening as a thank you for all your help. Shall we say eight o'clock?'

'That would be lovely,' said Hettie. They followed Fluff out of the marquee into the sunshine, leaving Mr Stickler to scowl at his labels. The preparations for the show were reaching fever pitch and there was a queue of cats waiting to consult Fluff about every conceivable hitch that had or might occur. Hettie watched as the landowner went about her business, assisting and reassuring as one problem after another was solved. The sad reality of what lay in the gatehouse had been pushed away for now and replaced by her dedication to the Wither-Fork legacy. She would no doubt deal with her sister's death when duty ceased to call, in quiet moments of deep regret.

The familiar figure of Blackberry Tibbs was making a beeline for Fluff, coming from the direction of the church and wearing a face like thunder. Hettie was intrigued, and she and Tilly moved forward to put themselves in earshot. 'They've gone, Miss!' cried Blackberry, trying to get her breath back. 'Some of my best work, just vanished without a trace.'

Fluff looked bewildered, but Tilly cottoned on straight away and nudged Hettie. 'I bet it's the scarecrows again.'

Blackberry overheard the comment and turned to Tilly. 'Yes, that's right. Someone's stolen the Wither-Forks from their pew – all four of them! And there's several missing from the allotments, as well.'

Practical as ever, Fluff intervened. 'Perhaps they'll turn up in time for the scarecrow procession tomorrow. If not, we'll think about putting on a scarecrow weekend for all your lovely figures. How does that sound?'

Blackberry was very taken with the idea of a special weekend dedicated to her work. Still feeling a little upset by the loss of her creations, but buoyed up by the prospect of her own show, she sidled back to the Hall to make some sandwiches for Fluff's lunch. Ever the detectives, Hettie and Tilly made for the church to check out the crime scene and wait for Bruiser.

The church was a hive of activity. There was a pungent smell of lilies as they entered, and Miss Jingle would clearly have a very tangible presence at the harvest festival service, but it was the altar that caught Hettie's eye. 'Just look at all that food,' she said, louder than she'd meant to.

Tilly gasped at the sight of such bounty. 'It's like Malkin and Sprinkle's food hall at Christmas,' she whispered. 'Just look at it all. Tins, packets, boxes, and look – whole hams and a giant pork pie! And the bread – sticks, baps and bloomers, and look at that one! It's a giant sheath of corn made from bread!'

The altar was a sight to behold, decorated to perfection with apples that had been polished until they shone, potatoes and carrots washed clean of any soil, and cabbages, cauliflowers and leeks, which all looked almost too perfect to be real. 'Looks lovely, doesn't it?' said Desiree Chit, emerging from the vestry. 'I was up till the small hours scrubbing them Maris Pipers – some of Rooster's best for years, and we had to keep the *really* good ones back for the judging. He's high hopes this year. Me and Apple have been setting this up all morning. Malkin and Sprinkle have sent some of Miss Jingle's lilies for the church out of respect, and they've made a lovely display by the pulpit – the festival wouldn't be the same without her flowers, especially as so many of them had to go up in smoke. Shame about Blackberry's scarecrows, though. They were here yesterday, cos Blight was having a chat with them. He thinks they're real, you see.'

Hettie looked across at the empty Wither-Fork pew, wondering why anyone would want to steal a bunch of medieval scarecrows. Desiree continued, changing the subject to one which Hettie had been hoping to avoid. 'Have you caught your murderer yet? I was only saying to Apple this morning, we just don't know what's going on up on the allotments. It's not a safe place to be with a killer on the loose. Have you detected who that might be?'

Hettie was saved by the Mulch sisters, who bustled through the church door behind a giant bunch of dahlias of every imaginable colour. 'Make way!' shouted Gladys, as her sister landed the flowers on the first available pew. 'We'll need a big vase for these. I hope you've left some space for us, Mrs Chit?'

Desiree stared with horror at the size of the dahlias. 'We've already got the lilies out, and I'm not sure where we can put those. The vases are full, so unless you stick them in the font you'll have to take them over to the Hall. Perhaps Miss Wither-Fork can find a home for them. Flowers were supposed to be here by nine this morning.'

Dahlia and Gladys exchanged a look that could easily have been murderous, and Gladys went in for the kill. 'Mrs Chit, might I remind you that during our father's time my sister and I were in sole charge of the floral arrangements for several churches in this parish, including St Kipper's, St Biscuit's, St Savoury's and St Wither-Fork's. I would ask you to move aside while we dress the altar with our blooms.'

Hettie and Tilly stood back and watched as Desiree Chit pulled herself up to her full height and addressed both Mulch sisters as one. 'And might I remind *you* of the chaos you caused last year during the harvest festival service, when your "blooms", as you call them, unleashed an army of earwigs into the congregation, causing a mass exodus during "We Plough the Fields and Scatter"! I repeat – the font's the best place for them. That way, any passengers they happen to be carrying will be closest to the door. As for your hold on the churches in the parish, mercifully that ended with the death of your dear father, who – by all accounts – wasn't particularly fond of earwigs either. Now, if you'll excuse me I have to get on.'

Hettie and Tilly managed to avoid the urge to applaud and made their way out of the church to find Bruiser. Time was getting on and – now they had an invitation to supper – Hettie thought it might be better to enjoy a Butters' pie for lunch, which would give her and Tilly an opportunity to make themselves presentable before returning to Wither-Fork for the harvest festival and their appointment with Fluff. On their way back to the gatehouse, where Miss Scarlet was parked, they passed the Reverend Augusta Stitch in her bread van, travelling at speed across the park. She was heading for the church, no doubt to check on the progress of her reluctant flock. 'I'd love to be an earwig on the wall when Desiree Chit, the Mulch sisters and the vicar from hell all converge in the left transept,' Hettie said. 'It's almost worth going back for.' The three friends' laughter rang out until they reached the gatehouse. Hettie stared up at the empty battlements with a pang of great sadness, half-expecting Micks Wither-Spoon to appear to give his Hamlet, but the ghosts were not long enough dead to cast their shadows, and the curtains had closed for the last time on that piece of theatre.

CHAPTER TWENTY-SIX

On arriving home, Bruiser treated himself to three sausage rolls and a ring doughnut from the bakery, and retired to a deckchair outside his shed for an afternoon nap. Hettie and Tilly, having devoured a Butters' steak pie and a cream horn each, set about choosing some suitable clothes for their evening out, but their filing cabinet was full of clothes that really didn't fit them any more. Since they'd set up home in the back room of Betty and Beryl's pie and pastry shop, their tabby waistlines had increased – but with the continuing success of the No. 2 Feline Detective Agency, they needed to smarten themselves up.

'It's going to have to be tabby chic again,' said

Tilly, sniffing a stain on the pocket of one of her best cardigans. 'I'll need to borrow Beryl's tin bath to give this lot a good soaking before the winter comes. I'm going to have to sponge this and hope that Fluff Wither-Fork doesn't notice. She did say informal, but I'm not sure stained, fusty cardigans count.'

Hettie stared at her own collection of best clothes, mostly made up of band-related T-shirts and a few remnants of stage gear from her days of touring. None of them fitted any more, but she clung to them as trophies of the glory days at the front of her folk rock band. She had been moderately successful with her music career, and these days she was even collectable among the more extreme progressive, psychedelic, acid-folk cat fans, as they liked to call themselves. Her new-age music had become almost old age, but the twelve-string guitar that rested on a beanbag in the corner of their room still got a regular workout when the mood was upon her, even if it did only have ten strings these days.

'Come on,' said Hettie, throwing the clothes back into the filing cabinet. 'Let's go and see what Jessie can offer us. The harvest festival doesn't start until six so we've plenty of time.'

Tilly clapped her paws with delight. A trip to her friend Jessie's charity shop was always a treat. Jessie had supplied most of Tilly's cardigans and, along with her benefactor, Miss Lambert, had saved Tilly from many a frosty night in the days when she was homeless. Miss Lambert now resided on Jessie's mantelpiece in a bright-red funeral urn, having left Jessie her small house and shop in Cheapcuts Lane.

Hettie and Tilly skipped down the high street, treating their shopping trip as a very welcome respite from the goings-on at Wither-Fork Hall. Jessie was in her window when they arrived, creating one of her themed displays. She bounded out to greet them. 'You two are a sight for tangled whiskers! I've had no gossip for weeks. What gives with our town's famous detectives? Any nice murders to report?'

Hettie gave Tilly a cautious look, then changed her mind. Jessie was discreet when she needed to be and had been a good friend to both of them in times of extreme difficulty. 'A bit of bother up at Wither-Fork Hall, actually. Four bodies and counting.'

Jessie's eyes threatened to pop out of her head as she turned the open sign to closed, dragging Hettie and Tilly into her back room for tea, biscuits and an overview of the latest case. An hour passed before the friends emerged to launch an assault on Jessie's clothes rails. Hettie went straight to a smart, black military-style jacket with a mandarin collar, and Tilly chose two cardigans – one in navy with an orange pocket for evening wear, and another in rainbow wool with a hood ready for the colder days to come. Pleased with their choices, Hettie went to pay, but Jessie waved the money away. 'Fair trade and all that,' she said. 'All that stuff on Wither-Fork! It's worth six cardies of anyone's money. I'm doing my window up to celebrate the Michaelmas Show, so perhaps I should include a few bodies in the concept. I wish I'd been there for the cremation – it sounds amazing, and much better than those awful funerals that Augusta Stitch puts on at St Kipper's. I popped in there the other day to say farewell to one of my old customers and there was no one in the church except the vicar and the coffin. It gave me a touch of agoraphobia, to be honest. Mind you, she certainly fills her pulpit. One of these days she'll get stuck in it, she's so fat.'

Hettie and Tilly roared with laughter. After their difficult days up at Wither-Fork Hall, Jessie and her view of life were just what they both needed – a proper tonic and some new clothes to wear. They said their goodbyes and left Jessie to dress her window for the Michaelmas Show.

The church of St Kipper's was set back at the bottom of the high street, opposite Malkin and Sprinkle, the town's department store. Hettie had never been inside before, but after what Jessie had said she was feeling curious. She loved the old graveyard, if only for the inscriptions on the stones, but going into the church had always been an unnecessary exercise. The large and opulent six-bedroomed rectory, which stood in close proximity, said everything that Hettie wanted to hear about religion. It was a stark contrast to the makeshift shelters that homeless cats set up around the town, in shop doorways, bus shelters and – if they were very lucky – old sheds.

They made their way down the path to the church and tried the big oak door, but it was locked. 'Bloody marvellous!' said Hettie. 'I suppose God's having his afternoon tea and can't be disturbed. No chance of a quick prayer, then. It's a disgrace – a great big barn like this, supposedly the centre of the community, and locked up like a pharaoh's tomb.'

'That's strange,' said Tilly, looking through the keyhole into the church. 'I think there's a service going on. There are several cats sitting in the pews at the front.'

Hettie bent down and took in the scene for herself. The line of vision through the keyhole was limited, but Tilly was right: she counted at least ten heads. 'They don't seem that bothered about being locked in. It's probably some sort of religious sect having a secret meeting. You know the sort – won't take aspirins if they've got a headache.'

'I don't think it's that sort of church,' said Tilly. 'But it *is* a lovely graveyard.'

Their ruminations on the state of St Kipper's came to an abrupt end when the air filled with diesel fumes and the Reverend Augusta Stitch brought her bread van to a standstill outside the rectory. Looking flustered, she crossed the graveyard to the church.

'What brings you here?' she asked. 'Our service doesn't start until seven-thirty this evening, as I'm doing the Wither-Fork harvest festival at six. Our evensong here at St Kipper's will be in the presence of His Highness, the Bishop. All are welcome, and the more the merrier. Do come back later and tell your friends. I'm hoping for a big turnout.'

Hettie was about to mention the present congregation closeted in the church, but Augusta Stitch was already pounding back across the graveyard to the rectory, where her bread van engine was still running. She and Tilly headed for home, pleased with their almost-new clothes and looking forward to their evening out; it was much better to be having a late supper with Fluff Wither-Fork than what might turn out to be the last supper with the Reverend Augusta Stitch.

Bruiser dropped Hettie and Tilly at the gates of Wither-Fork Hall in plenty of time for them to get a seat in the church. He'd arranged a tinkering session with Lazarus Hambone, who had acquired a number of old motorbikes to do up, and wasted no time in turning Miss Scarlet round and heading back into town, promising to return and pick them up at ten o'clock after their supper with Fluff.

The small church was bustling with cats and the evening sun shone through the stained-glass windows, throwing rainbows of light across the stone that concealed the Wither-Fork tomb. Morbid Balm was discreetly sizing up the job that Fluff had arranged with her for Monday: Micks and Mash were to be entombed together on a shelf away from the main family in a quiet and very private service, where Fluff would read a short eulogy before Morbid closed the lid on one of the most shameful aspects of the Wither-Forks' history to date. There had been plenty of murderers in days of old, when the Wither-Forks protected their lands, and even Lettuce herself had sentenced cats to death for stealing sheep to feed their families, but that was a very long time ago. These days it was better to sit round the table and discuss a way forward rather than bashing someone's brains out or favouring a ritualistic stabbing.

Hettie considered all of this as the congregation settled down ready for the service to begin. Fluff Wither-Fork was the last to arrive, and all stood as she entered the church and took her place in the empty Wither-Fork pew. There were one or two whispers as to the whereabouts of Micks and Mash, but everyone fell silent as Augusta Stitch entered the church from the vestry and made her way to the pulpit, nodding to Tarragon Trench in the organ loft to stop his selection of cantatas; Tarragon's response was laid-back. Augusta's signal had been clear enough, but the extra pipe of catnip he'd enjoyed before taking his place at the pedals had rather coloured his judgement on when and how to bring the music to an end. It was a further five minutes before Augusta was able to give her welcome address.

'All good gifts around us are sent from heaven above,' she began. 'And we are here to celebrate those gifts – the fruits of our labours, the toil of our lands, our good health and wealth from all the good things that God sees fit to share with us.' Hettie fidgeted as the vicar expounded on the premise that God owned everything and – by his judgement alone – some cats had it all and others had nothing. According to the doctrine coming from the pulpit, the meek would inherit the earth, but only as long as they behaved while they were starving or freezing to death. It was a great relief to her when Tarragon Trench eventually struck up the first notes to 'All Things Bright and Beautiful'.

The members of the congregation sang their hearts out as Tarragon added several extra verses. The vibration of the giant organ pipes and the enthusiastic caterwauling seemed to have released some of God's own creatures, and Hettie and Tilly watched the rapid progress of a legion of earwigs down the central aisle from the font where the Mulch sisters' dahlias had been abandoned. The pulpit had been festooned on either side by the late Miss Jingle's lilies, and these temptresses were attracting the earwigs, who were obviously bored with the flowers they were used to and were looking for pastures new. Tarragon finally brought the hymn to an end, allowing Augusta Stitch a window in which to offer some patronising advice to the gathered flock on how to live their lives if they wanted the all-important guarantee of eternal peace. The earwigs had a different plan, though, and took very little time in climbing the pulpit and infesting the vicar's clerical robes with their wriggling bodies in a bid to reach the lilies.

To say that Augusta Stitch ran from the church would be an understatement. She shrieked in horror, bounding out of the pulpit and beating off the earwigs with very little effect as they burrowed deep into her fur. To add more colour to the spectacle, Tarragon launched into a rock version of 'We Plough the Fields and Scatter', giving rise to some energetic dancing from Blight Chit, who had escaped his mother's paws and was now step-dancing up the mountain of foods displayed on the altar. Inevitably there was a landslide, and but for the quick-thinking of Jeremiah Corbit, Blight might have been buried alive. Corbit sprang from his pew, snatching the kitten from disaster as an avalanche of tinned pilchards, corned beef and spam rained down on him. The gallant action brought a round of applause from the pews and a grateful hug from Desiree, as Blight was put into Rooster's arms for safekeeping. Embarrassed, but secretly pleased to be a hero, Jeremiah slunk back to his seat, savouring the joys of being nice for a change and promising himself to try it more often.

'Now, that's what I call a church service,' said Hettie. 'If they were all like this I'd sign up.'

Tilly giggled as Fluff Wither-Fork rose from her family pew and climbed the steps into the pulpit, raising her paw to silence the congregation. Even Tarragon brought the organ music to an abrupt stop in deference to a higher authority, and all eyes turned to their benefactor. 'It has been a deeply sad week here at Wither-Fork Hall,' she began. 'Two terrible murders and now, for me, more grief than I care to mention. I would just like to assure you all that the horror and uncertainty are over, and you can sleep peacefully in your beds once again.' Fluff paused to allow her words to sink in, knowing that some would make a connection with the absence of Micks and Mash in the church. She shared a knowing look with Hettie and Tilly, and continued, 'On her death, Miss Jingle left a very generous legacy to Wither-Fork Hall, which means that we are saved from extinction. I intend to have Gertrude's allotment replanted with lilies and kept as a quiet place of contemplation and remembrance to her. I'm hoping that some of you would like to help with this project. There will be changes at Wither-Fork, but I promise that none of you will be turned away. I intend to build on the legacy that my ancestor, Lettuce Wither-Fork, bequeathed to us, enriching our community with a real sense of purpose. I hope you will all enjoy the Michaelmas Show and welcome the visitors who will flood through the gates tomorrow. Let's put this terrible week behind us and move on to better and more prosperous days.'

Fluff's rallying call was far better than any sermon the Reverend Stitch could have delivered, and as she climbed down from the pulpit her tenants clapped their paws together in appreciation. Tarragon Trench offered a boisterous rendition of 'The Arrival of the Queen of Sheba' as Fluff made her way down the central aisle and out of the church, signalling that the harvest festival was over for another year.

'Thank God for that!' said Hettie. 'I thought we were going to be stuck in here for hours listening to Augusta Stitch going off on one. I could hug the Mulch sisters for providing such a strong deterrent to her brand of Christianity. Long live the earwigs!'

Tilly giggled at her friend's outburst. Hettie Bagshot in a church would always be a risky business for those who went there to be pious, but Wither-Fork Church had taken on a party atmosphere now that God's messenger was picking earwigs out of her fur at the back of her bread van. Fluff had lifted their spirits and promised them all a future. There was much to discuss in the pews as the excited chatter rose in volume, competing with Tarragon Trench, who was now giving a very fine performance of baroque lollipops.

The Reverend Augusta Stitch finally managed to divest herself of her unwanted visitors. Not wishing to be late for the bishop, she drove at speed across the parkland en route to evensong at St Kipper's.

CHAPTER TWENTY-SEVEN

With a little time to spare before their supper engagement, Hettie and Tilly amused themselves by wandering through the stalls and tents of the Michaelmas Show. The atmosphere was electric as the cats who came every year to sell their wares gathered together to exchange news in small groups, smoking their catnip pipes and putting the world to rights. Bonny Grubb had renewed her acquaintance with a group of Gypsy toms who were running a set of swingboats, and they all sat on the grass enjoying Bonny's moonshine and regaling her with tales of life on the road.

The Chits were making their way back to the

allotments, with Blight perched on Rooster's shoulders, demolishing a candy floss that was twice as big as he was. Apple Chutney was putting the finishing touches to her stall of preserves, helped by Jeremiah Corbit, who seemed to have gone through some sort of transformation since saving a life in the church. Hettie stopped in front of the Hall and stared at the huge red sun as it sank slowly on the horizon, burnishing the parkland with a strange light. 'Perfect night for *Macbeth*,' she said. 'Just look at that blood-red sky.'

'It's a shame it all had to end in such a sad way,' said Tilly wistfully. 'I thought Micks and Mash were good fun, and I'd love to have seen their *Macbeth*.'

'It's all down to protecting your own, though, isn't it?' observed Hettie. 'When Mash saw the extent of the carnage in Gertrude Jingle's summer house, she knew that it was all over for both of them. She thought she'd got away with Bartlet's murder, but Micks compounded the problem by the frenzied killing of his mother. There was no way back after that.'

The church clock struck eight, and Hettie and Tilly turned towards the Hall to be met at the door by Blackberry Tibbs. 'Miss Wither-Fork's in her parlour this evening,' she said, as they followed her through the Great Hall and down the stone steps to the servant's quarters. No sooner were they in the corridor than Hettie detected a strong smell of roasted chicken. She quickened her pace, hoping that Fluff's supper table would offer some proper food for a change, and she wasn't disappointed: Fluff stood with carving knife in paw, ready to cut into the large chicken, which took up half the space on her small parlour table.

At Fluff's invitation, Hettie and Tilly sat down and watched as three plates were filled with hot slices of chicken. Blackberry made several journeys from the kitchen to add to the feast with a bowl of creamy mashed potatoes, a large jug of gravy and a baking tray of little sausages wrapped in bacon. Hettie was thrilled to see that there wasn't a green vegetable in sight. 'I thought the least we could do was to offer you a decent meal after all your hard work,' said Fluff, passing the plates to her guests. 'In Lettuce Wither-Fork's time there would have been a grand banquet in the great hall on Michaelmas Eve, with minstrels, jugglers and players; now, we just have an empty fireplace and buckets, but I think it's time that all that changed for the better. Please help yourselves to potatoes and sausages.'

Hettie didn't need a second invitation, but helped her friend first, seeing the potential of an overspill of creamy mash onto Fluff's clean white tablecloth if Tilly's large paws connected with the bowl. The food was excellent, and there was very little conversation until Blackberry returned from the kitchen to collect plates that had been licked clean. She returned minutes later with a giant lemon meringue pie and a jug of cream.

Tilly couldn't resist clapping her paws with delight, and Fluff and Hettie laughed at her enthusiasm. Fluff cut into the pie, releasing a tangy aroma of lemons and cooked pastry, and Tilly reacted by dribbling ever so slightly down the front of her nearly new best cardigan. No one noticed, and the three cats tucked in until they were defeated, leaning back in their chairs to recover from what Hettie would describe later as 'a full-on culinary experience'.

Blackberry returned to clear the table, and Fluff invited Hettie and Tilly to join her by the fire. The supper conversation had been light and inconsequential, punctuated by the odd grunt of appreciation for the food, but Hettie knew that Fluff Wither-Fork was merely playing for time before revealing the real reason for her invitation. The landowner looked over at the table where Blackberry was busy stacking the pots. 'Thank you, Blackberry – that was an excellent dinner. Please leave the washing-up until tomorrow, and take some chicken and pudding home with you. We have an early start, as the bakers will be arriving with their entries, and no doubt Mr Stickler will be on the edge of his annual nervous breakdown, so we'll need all paws on deck.'

Blackberry put the stack of pots on a tray and left Fluff to her guests, closing the parlour door behind her. Fluff waited for the sound of her footsteps to recede, followed by the bang of the front door as she let herself out. 'Now, then,' she said. 'I expect you're wondering why I've asked you both here tonight.' Hettie nodded, and Tilly moved further forward on the sofa, giving Fluff her full attention. Fluff paused, as if choosing the right words, and finally spoke. 'I'm not proud of what my sister did to that poor cat from the National Crust, but I can see why, and I feel very responsible for driving her to it. In her way, she was protecting the cat she loved. She knew that Micks wouldn't want to move from the gatehouse, and she also knew that he was fragile and had certain . . . tendencies, shall we say, if he became distressed.' Hettie was tempted to interject. 'Certain tendencies' was a very strange phrase to describe viciously stabbing several cats to death, but she allowed Fluff to continue, 'I feel they have both paid the ultimate price for what they did, and I was wondering whether you might consider what I believe they call in detective fiction a "cover-up"?'

Of all the possible scenarios, Hettie wouldn't have predicted this one. 'You mean blame the murders on someone else?' she said.

'Yes, I think that's what I mean. You see, no one knows yet that Micks and Mash were involved. The only other cat who is even aware of their deaths is Morbid Balm, and she doesn't know why they died. To save the face of the Wither-Forks, I was wondering whether you might be willing and able to come up with a suitable alternative regarding the murders?'

Hettie's mind was racing. The strange request was completely understandable, but it turned the whole case upside down. It would be very unfair to accuse another cat of the crimes, and manufacturing one lie meant that so many more would have to follow. She was about to voice her thoughts when Tilly entered the conversation. 'We could say it was all to do with the maharaja and one of those nasty marbled cats who stole Miss Jingle's palace and murdered Mr Jodpurr,' she suggested. 'I know she escaped from them, but perhaps we could say they caught up with her in the end.'

Fluff looked confused. Hettie had given her only a very brief outline of Gertrude Jingle's past history, and Tilly's idea sounded like something straight out of one of Mr Kipling's adventure stories. 'I think that sounds a little far-fetched, if you don't mind my saying so. The story would have to be believable.'

Tilly looked crushed by Fluff's response, but Hettie wasn't as dismissive. 'Actually, I think Tilly might be on to something there,' she said. 'It was a possibility we considered at one point, and to make things work we need to concentrate on the idea of strangers who come, do their worst and disappear without a trace. The thought of some exotic bunch of cut-throat cats out for revenge might be exactly what's needed here – although it doesn't explain why they would kill Bartlet Crustworthy if they were after Miss Jingle.'

Tilly, Hettie and Fluff all stared into the fire, waiting for inspiration to strike. Once again it was Tilly who came up with a possible solution. 'We could say that the marbled cat was lying in wait on Bonny's allotment and was disturbed by Bartlet. The nasty cat bashes Bartlet over the head and goes back into hiding, waiting for an opportunity to strike at Miss Jingle, which he does the following night. Then he escapes before anyone knows what's happened.'

Fluff clapped her paws together. 'Bravo, Miss Jenkins! That sounds perfect.'

Hettie looked less certain, raising a few issues that Tilly hadn't considered. 'The big question is – how do we know all this? At some stage we're going to have to explain to Binky Crustworthy how and why her brother was murdered. I wonder if she'll be willing to accept the Bollywood gangland scenario.'

'She will if we tell her that it's simply a case of being in the wrong place at the wrong time. It's kinder than saying Mash bashed his head in because she didn't want the National Crust to take over the estate,' said Tilly, defending her idea. 'We could even give the murderer a name. We could call him Deepak Rishabh, like the leader of the marbled cats – that's a marvellous name for a murderer. I wrote it down in my notebook because I liked it so much.'

Hettie couldn't resist a smile. Tilly loved a good story and her enthusiasm for making things up was proving to be quite an asset, but there was still one big stumbling block which impacted on the professional reputation of the No. 2 Feline Detective Agency. 'But how do we know all this? Without any evidence, I don't see how the story can be credible.'

Hettie and Fluff both looked at Tilly, waiting once again for the oracle to speak. They weren't disappointed. 'Miss Jingle!' said Tilly. 'We can say we found a threatening note in her suitcase. You know, something like "You're dead", or "You must die", or even "I know who you are". We could say that we made the connection through the newspaper cuttings we found about the maharaja's murder, and that it was only a matter of time before Miss Jingle went the same way.'

Fluff looked at Hettie this time, waiting for her approval. Hettie stared into the fire, remembering the serenity of Miss Jingle's cremation and how keen she had been in her letter to protect Micks from himself and Mash from Micks. Eventually, she spoke. 'OK, if we go with Tilly's story I think the best way to deal with it is to give away as little as possible. We should say that Miss Jingle was murdered by a cat from her past life in India. We could also say that Bartlet Crustworthy disturbed him while he was looking at the allotments, which makes Bartlet into a bit of a hero, dying in the act of apprehending a would-be killer. I'd be happy to report that to Binky Crustworthy. Thinking about it, I'm sure Miss Jingle would approve of our keeping Micks and Mash out of the picture. Strangely, she was to blame for most of the murders, anyway. If she hadn't abandoned Micks, he wouldn't have killed Scoop and Lorrie Wither-Spoon or the cat at his drama school. By then, he'd got a taste for blood. It must have been easy for him to do it again after he'd discovered Miss Jingle's deceit. He clearly expected his ivory tower to protect him – and it did, in a funny sort of way.'

'What do you mean?' asked Fluff.

'Well, Mash was his ivory tower – she protected him from the outside world. That's why she killed Bartlet Crustworthy – because he was a threat to their way of life. She killed Micks because he was a threat to himself, and she knew that there was no escape for her.'

It was Fluff's turn to stare into the fire as the tears that had refused to come filled her eyes and ran down her face. The stoic facade was washed away by a deep sense of loss for her sister and the cat she had died for, and any doubts Hettie had about the cover-up melted away at the sight of her grief. Fluff's body shook with a pain for which there would be no cure. She would have to live with the part she had played in the deception, but, to the outside world, the reputation of Mash Wither-Spoon and the Wither-Forks would remain intact.

Several minutes and three very soggy tissues later,

Fluff managed to compose herself sufficiently to offer her gratitude to Hettie and Tilly. She stood up and moved to her desk at the other end of the parlour, returning with a bundle of notes and counting fifty pounds into Hettie's paw. 'This doesn't seem enough for what you're willing to do for me. If you think I should pay more, then you must say. I will never forget your kindness, and there will always be a welcome for you here at Wither-Fork Hall.'

'Fifty pounds is very acceptable,' said Hettie, suppressing the urge to dance triumphantly around Fluff Wither-Fork's parlour. The way things were going, she and Tilly would be able to hibernate all winter without lifting a paw, and have a good Christmas into the bargain. They were more than happy to prosper from Fluff's bribe for their alternative version of The Michaelmas Murders. There was, however, one question that Hettie felt she had to ask. 'What about Micks and Mash? How will you explain their deaths to the cats on the estate?'

Fluff sat down again and warmed her paws by the fire. 'I think it best if I stick mostly to the truth,' she said. 'The tenants are very aware of Micks' eccentricities. I shall tell them that he managed to poison himself accidently during one of his theatrical capers, and that Mash couldn't live without him so decided to go the same way. Suicide is still regarded as a sin by some, so I shall ask for their discretion in keeping Mash's reputation untarnished. I've arranged a private interment with Morbid Balm in our family tomb at the church for Monday, and I will inform the tenants after that.'

Hettie admired the cool and assured way in which Fluff Wither-Fork had arrived at her own personal arrangements, and considered that Fluff herself, under different circumstances, would have made a clever murderer and a very tricky adversary. This time round, everything seemed to be in place for a getting-away-with-it-by-the-skin-of-your-teeth ending. 'You mentioned in church that there were some changes on the way here at Wither-Fork,' said Hettie, lightening the conversation.

'I did, and not before time. Miss Jingle's money will enable me to fix the Hall and restore it to its former glory, but we need to look to the future and make sure we sustain her legacy. My gardens and the Michaelmas Show don't bring in enough income. We need to attract visitors all year round, so I've decided to make the tenants work for their places here at Wither-Fork. It's not good enough for them to potter about on their allotments, providing a few vegetables and flowers. In Lettuce Wither-Fork's time, they had to work the land and serve in the Hall, so that's my plan. I'm going to open Wither-Fork to visitors and create a theatre space in the Great Hall, which I shall dedicate to Micks and Mash. We shall have evening performances from travelling companies all year round, and I shall move to the gatehouse where I can keep an eye on things. The tenants will be asked to work in the gardens or in the Hall, depending on their skills. Only those too old to work will be spared. We have to justify our existence, and Miss Jingle's generous legacy has given us the chance to do that.'

Hettie and Tilly were impressed, and said so as their evening out drew to a close. Tucking the fifty pounds into the pocket of her almost-new jacket, Hettie rose from the sofa, and she and Tilly escaped into the cool night air.

CHAPTER TWENTY-EIGHT

The parkland was lit by lanterns as Hettie and Tilly emerged from Wither-Fork Hall. The cats who were part of the show were making preparations for bed in their tents and vans as the chilly September night drove them in from their conversations under the stars. It was a magical sight as the lanterns were extinguished one by one, leaving only a few late-night cats to mull over the day's events.

Hettie and Tilly took the path that led directly to the gatehouse. They had ten minutes to spare before Bruiser was due, but once again their progress was rudely interrupted by the roar of Augusta Stitch's bread van as it forced its way across the park, heading in the direction of the church. Hettie grabbed Tilly, pulling her off the path as the van thundered past and left a plume of black diesel smoke behind it. Tilly choked, waving the fumes away with her paw, and Hettie stared after the van. 'I wonder what she's up to at this time of night?' she said. 'We've got a few minutes before Bruiser gets here. Come on, let's have a look.'

The friends retraced their steps and took the path to the church, which was in darkness. The van had disappeared around the back and, as they approached, they could clearly see a flashlight moving about in the dark. They stood silently at the corner of the church, watching as the back doors of the van were thrown open to reveal what appeared to be a mountain of dead bodies, stacked on top of each other. The substantial form of Augusta Stitch dragged the bodies out of the van, wheezing with the effort, and took them one by one through the back door of the church.

Hettie signalled to Tilly to stay put as she crept towards the van, which was now empty. Minutes later, Augusta emerged with an armful of tins as Hettie dissolved into a convenient rose bush. The vicar repeated her journey several times, filling the back of her van with the food from the harvest festival altar. When she could fit no more in, she closed the doors and moved round to the driver's seat, where Hettie pounced. 'Good evening, Vicar,' she began. 'A nice evening for a spot of undercover work?'

Augusta was so taken by surprise that she was speechless, and stood staring blankly at Hettie before recovering herself. 'It's not what it looks like,' she said. 'It's part of my pastoral duties. All this food has to be distributed to the poor of the parishes, and I thought I'd get an early start in the morning. God waits for no cat, you know.'

Hettie was pleased to see that the Reverend Stitch was visibly shaken and decided to go in for the kill. 'And what about the bodies you've just unloaded into the church? Are they the poor of the parish or part of your congregation at St Kipper's? Have you bored them to death with your patronising dogma? You might have fooled your bishop, but you won't get one over on me!'

'No, no! You don't understand,' she said defensively. 'They're not dead, they're . . .'

'Scarecrows!' shouted Tilly triumphantly, joining Hettie by the van.

Augusta Stitch was crushed. She had been caught fair and square, and had nothing to say in her defence. She fell to her knees, offering a woeful request for forgiveness up into the evening sky as Hettie and Tilly began to unload the food and take it back into the church. The scarecrows had been roughly dumped by the Wither-Fork pew. Tilly counted at least a dozen of

Blackberry's beautifully crafted figures, so recently used to bulk out St Kipper's congregation. She was pleased that they had been returned in time for the show, as it was one of the attractions she'd been most looking forward to. Now, the scarecrow procession and competition could go ahead, and seemingly there was no harm done – but not even divine intervention could save the Reverend Stitch. When all the tins, fruit and vegetables had been safely rescued from her clutches, Hettie felt that an explanation was due to her.

The vicar was sobbing by one of the back wheels of her van as Hettie and Tilly approached. 'Not exactly typical behaviour for a cat of the cloth,' Hettie began. 'Kidnapping scarecrows and stealing food from the poor. I would think that's a hanging offence in your line of business.'

'You don't understand,' said Augusta. 'I was forced into it. My congregations have been dwindling and the bishop gave me a final warning – either I improve my ratings or I'd be banished to the chapter house to wait at table like a servant. I thought if I added the scarecrows to the front of the church, he'd think I'd pulled things together and let me stay, but one of the heads fell off during the Lord's Prayer and I was undone.'

Tilly stifled a giggle, and Augusta continued, 'I've never seen the bishop so angry. He went round the whole congregation to see which cats were real and which weren't, and he didn't even let me finish the service. He marched me back to the rectory and defrocked me there and then. He said there was no place for liars and cheats in his diocese and gave me twenty-four hours to pack up and leave. I've lost my home and my job. I knew that I should return the scarecrows, and I was tempted by all that food in the church. With no livelihood to sustain me, I'm afraid I helped myself, and now I'm at your mercy.'

Hettie looked at the shambling wreck in front of her. It had been a day of compromises, a day when the truth hadn't always been the best course of action. Augusta Stitch had never been the ideal candidate to serve the spiritual needs of her allotted flock, and the bishop's silver lining to Augusta's cloud was perhaps a real blessing. 'I'm with the bishop,' said Hettie. 'I think your time is done here. You should go where you can find something real to believe in instead of hiding behind a dog collar that chokes you. Good luck and goodbye.'

Augusta looked into Hettie's face, and for the first time in her life felt the warmth of a kindness and understanding that she had never been able to find in her Bible. It was a revelation to her to feel free and alive without looking to the heavens. As she climbed into her van, she knew that her life would from then on be governed by earthly matters, and she embraced the many joys that they would bring.

'Had you thought of applying for the vacancy?' asked Tilly as they waved Augusta off.

'I'm not sure that the Reverend Bagshot has the right ring about it,' said Hettie, and led the way to the gatehouse, where Bruiser was waiting with Miss Scarlet.

ACKNOWLEDGEMENTS

The joy of having my own allotment has done much to inspire this book. Many of the characters are taken from life, and with that in mind I would like to thank Lady Victoria Leatham, Fenella Dawn and the National Trust.

A big thank you also to Susie Dunlop and all at Allison and Busby, W. F. Howes and Jenny Funnell, and St Martin's Press across the Pond, who have all made this series of books a reality, and to Marni and Arthur for their belief and support.

Finally, Nicola, who shares every journey and adventure with our lovely girls, Hettie and Tilly, who may be gone, but are never forgotten.

MANDY MORTON began her professional life as a musician. More recently, she has worked as a freelance arts journalist for national and local radio. She currently presents the radio arts magazine *The Eclectic Light Show* and lives with her partner, who is also a crime writer, in Cambridge and Cornwall, where there is always a place for an ageing long-haired tabby cat.

@icloudmandy
@hettiebagshot
HettieBagshotMysteries

Hettie Bagshot has bitten off more than any cat could chew. As soon as she launches her No. 2 Feline Detective Agency, she's bucketed into a case: Furcross, home for slightly older cats, has a nasty spate of bodysnatching, and three of the residents have been stolen from their graves. Hettie and her sidekick, Tilly, set out to reveal the terrible truth. Is Nurse Mogadon involved in a deadly game? And what flavour will Betty Butter's pie of the week be?

In a haze of catnip and pastry, Hettie steers the Furcross Case to its conclusion, but will she get there before the body count rises – and the pies sell out?

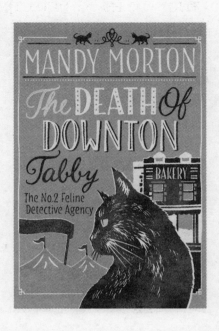

The town is celebrating its first literary festival, and The No. 2 Feline Detective Agency has been hired to oversee security.

On the arrival of the three Brontë sisters and the famous aristocat, Sir Downton Tabby, Hettie Bagshot and her sidekick, Tilly, are plunged into crisis as a serial killer stalks the festival grounds. Will there be an author left standing? Will Meridian Hambone sell out of her 'Littertray' T-shirts? And will there be enough Crime Teas to go round?

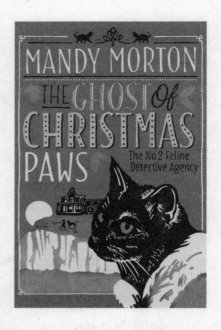

It's a week before Christmas and Hettie and Tilly set out on a very dangerous case for The No. 2 Feline Detective Agency. Lady Eloise Crabstock-Singe has summoned them to the Cornish coast to solve the mystery of Christmas Paws: a servant cat who haunts the family manor intent on killing off all of the Crabstocks.

Should they put their trust in Absalom and Lamorna Tweek? Will Saffron Bunn's cooking get any better? And will Hettie and Tilly get home safely in time for Christmas dinner?

To discover more great books and to
place an order visit our website at
allisonandbusby.com

Don't forget to sign up to our free newsletter at
allisonandbusby.com/newsletter
for latest releases, events and exclusive offers

 Allison & Busby Books
 @AllisonandBusby

You can also call us on
020 7580 1080
for orders, queries
and reading recommendations